POLAR WILDLIFE

Kamini Khanduri

Scientific consultant: Sheila Anderson

Contents

Polar areas

The two polar areas, the Arctic and the Antarctic, are the coldest places on Earth. The temperature hardly ever rises above freezing point so the land and the sea are frozen for most of the year. In summer, the sun never sets. In winter, the sun never rises so it is dark all day and night. Despite this, many kinds of wildlife manage to survive in polar areas. You can find out about some of them in this book.

Strange lights, called auroras, appear in the sky above polar areas.

Ice and snow

It is so cold in polar areas that the snow that falls there does not all melt. The snow that remains is pressed into ice by the next snowfall. Over hundreds of years, a thick layer of ice has built up. In some places, it is 3km (nearly 2 miles) thick. The ice does not stay in one place. As more snow pushes down on it, it moves slowly downhill to the sea. This moving ice is called a glacier.

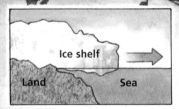

When glaciers reach the sea, they often keep moving outward. They make a platform of ice which floats on the surface of the sea but is still attached to the land. This is called an ice shelf.

In winter, ice forms on the surface of polar seas. This sea ice, or pack ice, is solid enough to walk on. Patches of pack ice, called floes, join together into huge sheets.

Pancake ice is a kind of pack ice. It is made up of small floes of soft ice. As the floes bump against each other, their edges curl upward, so they look like pancakes (see left).

The Arctic

The Arctic is made up of the Arctic Ocean and the land around it. This land is called the tundra. No trees grow on the tundra because it is so cold and windy, but smaller plants grow there in summer. Many animals live in the Arctic. Snowy owls and Arctic foxes live on the tundra, polar bears live on the pack ice and seals and whales live in the sea. Many birds spend the summer in the Arctic.

This map shows the Arctic from above. You can see the northern parts of the countries around the Arctic Ocean. On maps, an imaginary line called the Arctic Circle surrounds the Arctic area.

The Antarctic

The Antarctic is made up of a continent called Antarctica, the Southern Ocean around it and the islands in the Southern Ocean. The land in the Antarctic is colder than the land in the Arctic because it is closer to the pole. Few plants can grow there and the largest animal that lives on the land is a tiny insect. In the sea, though, there are seals and whales. Many birds, such as penguins, get their food from the sea.

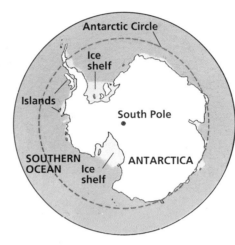

This map shows the Antarctic, with the imaginary line, the Antarctic Circle, around it. Antarctica is one-and-a-half times the size of the USA and nearly 60 times the size of Britain.

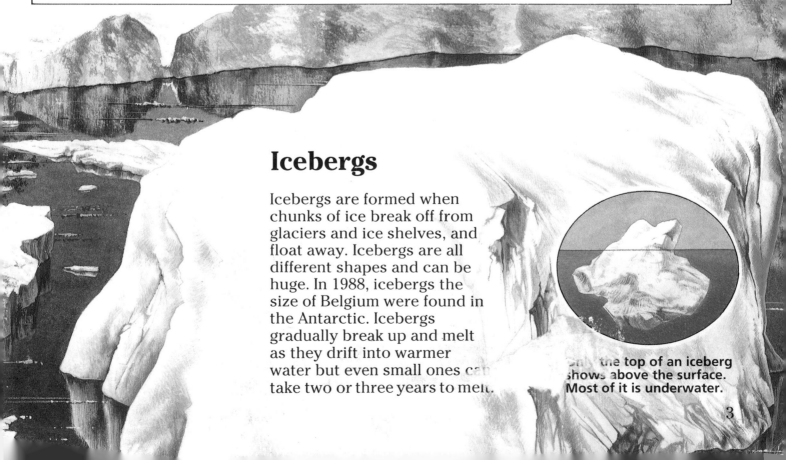

Icebergs

Icebergs are formed when chunks of ice break off from glaciers and ice shelves, and float away. Icebergs are all different shapes and can be huge. In 1988, icebergs the size of Belgium were found in the Antarctic. Icebergs gradually break up and melt as they drift into warmer water but even small ones can take two or three years to melt.

Only the top of an iceberg shows above the surface. Most of it is underwater.

3

Polar bears

Polar bears live in the Arctic. They are the largest bears in the world - nearly twice as tall as a person and ten times as heavy. Polar bears do not stay in one place. They make long journeys across deep snow and slippery ice, looking for different kinds of food. They eat seals, birds, fish and plants. Adult polar bears spend most of their lives on their own. Baby polar bears are called cubs. They stay with their mother while they are young.

Polar bears spend a lot of time swimming in the icy Arctic Ocean.

Polar bears are kept warm by their thick fur coats and by a layer of fat under their skin. The only parts of their bodies which are not covered in fur are their noses and the pads under their paws.

When cubs are born, they are so tiny, their mother can hide them in between the toes of her front paws. Cubs grow quickly - in one year, they are as big as a person.

Inside the den

Polar bears give birth to their cubs in dens in the snow, to protect them from the cold and wind. The cubs stay in the den for about three months. The mother feeds them with her own milk, but eats nothing herself.

Hole for air

Main chamber

Cubs' chamber

Entrance tunnel

Up to 3 cubs are born at one time.

Some dens have a lower chamber.

After leaving the den, mother and cubs stay together for about two years. She teaches them to hunt, so they can look after themselves.

Bear tracking

Scientists can learn more about how polar bears spend their lives by following, or tracking, their movements. To do this, they put a bear to sleep for a short time and fit it with a collar which has a radio transmitter on it. When the bear wakes up, its movements can be tracked by a satellite in space.

This scientist is putting a radio collar on to a drugged polar bear.

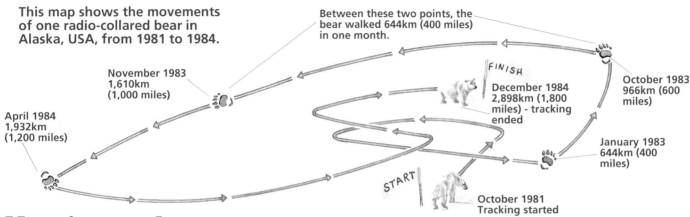

This map shows the movements of one radio-collared bear in Alaska, USA, from 1981 to 1984.

Between these two points, the bear walked 644km (400 miles) in one month.

FINISH
December 1984
2,898km (1,800 miles) - tracking ended

November 1983
1,610km
(1,000 miles)

October 1983
966km (600 miles)

April 1984
1,932km
(1,200 miles)

January 1983
644km (400 miles)

START
October 1981
Tracking started

Hunting seals

A polar bear's main food is ringed seals. The pictures on the right show how a bear snatches a seal from its breathing hole in the pack ice.

The bear approaches the hole quietly, so the seal does not hear the vibrations of its feet through the ice.

The bear lies in wait, without moving, for up to 4 hours, until a seal's head pokes out of the hole.

The bear quickly kills the seal, using its paws and teeth. It then pulls it out of the water and eats it.

Bears in town

Arctic Circle

Churchill

Hudson Bay

CANADA

On their journeys, some polar bears pass near a town called Churchill, in Canada. They search for food at a rubbish dump outside the town and sometimes go right into town. Schoolchildren in Churchill have lessons in bear safety.

The dump is dangerous for bears. They may eat harmful rubbish or choke on bits of plastic.

Living in polar seas

In polar areas, there is more wildlife living in the sea than on the land. It is hard to survive on the land because it is so cold and windy. Polar seas are cold too, but there is no wind underwater and the temperature does not change much. On these pages, you can see some of the plants and animals which live in the Southern Ocean, around Antarctica.

In winter, the surface of the Southern Ocean is covered by a layer of pack ice. This ice may be as thick as 3m (nearly 10ft). Pack ice moves around as the water beneath it moves. It is also blown by the wind.

Plankton

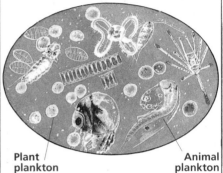

Plant plankton

Animal plankton

Plankton are tiny plants and animals found in all seas. They are very important because so many larger animals, from small fish to huge whales, feed on them. Plankton float near the surface because the plants need sunlight to grow.

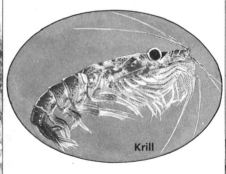

Krill

Krill are a type of animal plankton. Huge numbers live in the Southern Ocean. If all the krill in the world were put together, they would weigh more than all the people.

On the sea-bed

In shallow parts of polar seas, the ice on the surface scrapes against the sea-bed as the tide rises and falls. This makes it hard for animals to live there. In deeper water, the ice does not reach the bottom, so many animals live on the sea-bed. They feed on each other, or on dead plankton which falls from above.

Anemone

Starfish

Sponge

Sea slug

Sea spider

Sea urchin

Sea cucumber

Unusual fish

Some Antarctic fish have special ways of surviving in very cold water.

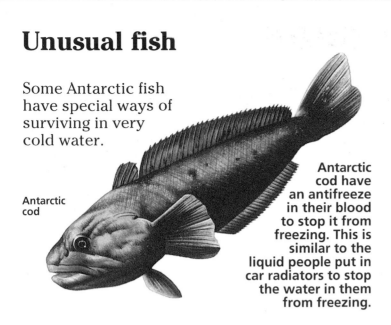

Antarctic cod

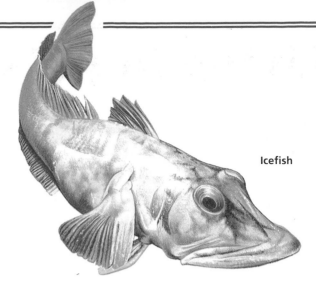

Icefish

Antarctic cod have an antifreeze in their blood to stop it from freezing. This is similar to the liquid people put in car radiators to stop the water in them from freezing.

Icefish have no red blood cells. Most animals need these red cells because they carry extra oxygen around their bodies. In very cold water, blood can carry enough oxygen without the red cells.

Underwater food web

Wherever they live, animals depend on plants, or on other animals, for food. One way of showing who eats what is by a food web. This picture shows an Antarctic underwater food web. (The pictures are not to scale.)

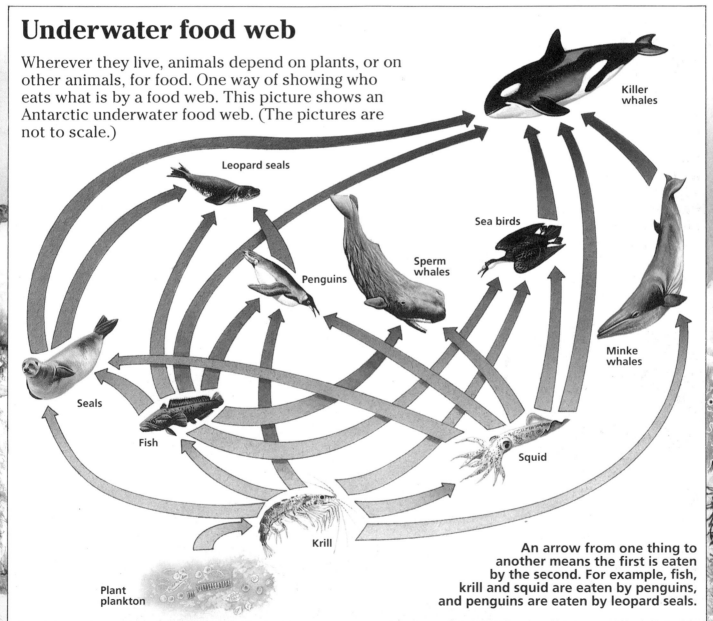

Leopard seals

Penguins

Sperm whales

Sea birds

Killer whales

Minke whales

Seals

Fish

Squid

Krill

Plant plankton

An arrow from one thing to another means the first is eaten by the second. For example, fish, krill and squid are eaten by penguins, and penguins are eaten by leopard seals.

7

Penguins

Penguins are sea birds which cannot fly. They all live in the southern half of the world and seven species live in the Antarctic (see below). Penguins are kept warm by two layers of short, tightly-packed feathers and by a layer of fat under their skin.

Although they cannot fly, penguins are very good swimmers and divers. They use their stiff, narrow wings as flippers in the water. Antarctic penguins spend most of their lives swimming in the icy Southern Ocean, catching fish, squid and krill.

Penguins only leave the sea at breeding times. They come on to land, or ice, and make their way to their breeding places, which are called rookeries. Year after year, penguins return to the rookery where they were hatched. They often return to the same mate, too.

This emperor penguin is keeping its chick warm. The chick stands on its parent's feet and snuggles under a special flap of skin. Both males and females have this flap of skin.

Penguins use their special flap of skin to keep their eggs warm.

Penguin sizes

In these pictures, you can see how tall the seven Antarctic penguins are.

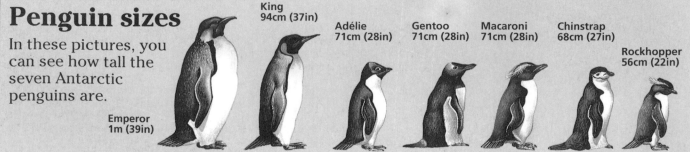

King 94cm (37in)

Adélie 71cm (28in)

Gentoo 71cm (28in)

Macaroni 71cm (28in)

Chinstrap 68cm (27in)

Rockhopper 56cm (22in)

Emperor 1m (39in)

Ice-breeding emperors

Most birds breed in summer. Emperor penguins breed in winter on the cold, windy pack ice around Antarctica. These pictures show what happens.

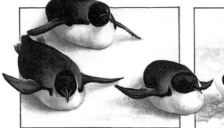

The penguins leave the water and walk across the ice to their rookeries - a journey of up to 160km (100 miles).

On sloping ground, penguins toboggan along on their fronts, pushing themselves forward with their flippers.

At the rookery, penguins pair up and mate. Each female lays 1 egg, passes it to the male and goes back to the sea to feed.

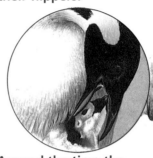

For up to 9 weeks, the male keeps the egg warm on his feet. He does not eat at all during this time so he gets very thin.

Groups of males huddle together for warmth, with their backs to the wind. They take turns on the outside.

Around the time the chick hatches, the female returns with food. The chick reaches inside her beak to feed.

Older chicks stand in groups, called crèches. Their parents feed them all winter. Then they look after themselves.

Crested penguins

Crested penguins are very fierce. They get their name because they have spiky, golden feathers above their eyes. These feathers are especially bright when the penguins are courting (looking for mates). There are two kinds of crested penguins living in the Antarctic - macaronis and rockhoppers.

These macaroni penguins are doing a courtship display. A male and female stand on their nest, calling to each other and waving their heads.

Macaroni penguins

Rockhopper penguins

Rockhopper penguin's head

Rockhopper penguins hop from rock to rock as they move up and down the steep cliffs above the sea where they make their nests.

Penguin nests

Penguins have very little nest-building material because so few plants grow in Antarctica. King and emperor penguins do not make nests at all. They lay their eggs on bare ground or ice. Other Antarctic penguins make nests by scraping a shallow hole in the ground and filling it with pebbles.

When a pair of Adélie penguins meet at their nest, they do a courtship dance before mating. They stand face to face, stretch their heads and necks upward and make loud, squawking calls. They beat their wings up and down slowly.

To keep their eggs warm, male and female Adélies take turns on the nest. When the pair change places, they often gather more pebbles to add to the nest.

Adélie penguins

Expert swimmers

Penguins often look clumsy when they are walking on land. In water, though, they are very graceful. They almost fly through the water and can stay under for up to 18 minutes.

Penguins jump or dive into the sea from ledges or cliffs.

Penguins swim fast underwater. They steer with their feet and tails and catch fish, squid and krill with their beaks.

Penguins often come flying out of the water to take a breath. They travel through the air at speeds of up to 25kph (16mph).

Sometimes, penguins swim slowly along on the surface, with their necks sticking up, like ducks or geese.

Leopard seal dangers

One of the greatest dangers to penguins is being caught by a leopard seal. These seals eat all kinds of penguins, but Adélies are their main food. These pictures show how a leopard seal catches an Adélie penguin in the water.

The leopard seal lies in wait in the water, hiding underneath a ledge of ice which juts out over the surface of the sea.

Adélie penguins gather on the ledge, on their way to feed in the sea. Those at the front start to jump into the water.

The leopard seal immediately darts out from its hiding place and grabs one of the penguins from behind.

The other penguins escape by swimming away, or by leaping out of the water, back to the safety of the ledge.

Following the sun

Scientists believe that Adélie penguins use the sun to help them find their rookeries. In an experiment, they moved a group of penguins 1,500km (930 miles) from their rookery and then followed their movements as the penguins tried to find their way back. The map on the right shows what happened.

Penguins started here. They set off in the wrong direction.

START

Sun came out - penguins walked in the right direction

To the rookeries

Sun came out again

Sun disappeared. Penguins lost sense of direction.

Route of penguins while sun was behind clouds.

Route of penguins while sun was shining.

Crowded rookeries

Rookeries are dirty, noisy places. Thousands of squawking, pecking penguins gather there at breeding times. Despite the crowds, each penguin knows its own mate or chick by calling to them, and by recognizing their answering call.

Adult king penguin

King penguin chick

This king penguin chick is turning into an adult. It is losing its fluffy, baby feathers and growing adult ones.

Land mammals

Mammals are animals which give birth to live babies, instead of laying eggs. Baby mammals feed on their mother's milk. Most mammals have hair or fur on their bodies. There are no land mammals in the Antarctic. On the next four pages, you can see some of the land mammals which live in the Arctic.

Caribou

Caribou are a type of deer. In Europe and Asia, they are called reindeer. They eat plants, such as lichens (see page 28). In winter, caribou live in forests on the edge of the Arctic. In spring, huge groups travel up to 1,000km (620 miles) north, to spend the summer feeding on the tundra. These journeys in search of food are called migrations.

A line of migrating caribou may stretch for 300km (186 miles). Caribou are strong swimmers so they can cross the rivers along their routes.

Caribou lose their antlers once a year and grow new ones. They are the only species of deer in which females, as well as males, have antlers.

Caribou can walk on deep snow because their wide hooves are fringed with fur, like snow-shoes.

Musk oxen

Musk oxen are related to goats. They live in the Arctic all year long, kept warm by their thick, shaggy fur coats. Musk oxen look clumsy, but, like goats, they are very sure-footed.

When they are in danger of being attacked by wolves, groups of musk oxen often huddle together in a line, with their fierce-looking horns facing the enemy.

Caribou use the same migration routes every year. In Alaska, USA, an oil pipeline has been laid across these routes. The pipeline is raised above the ground, so the caribou can walk under it.

Oil pipeline

Wolves

Top of the order

Bottom of the order

Wolves live in groups, called packs, of up to 20 members. Each wolf has its place in the pack's order of importance. You can tell how important a wolf is by the way it behaves, and by its body shape. The pictures on the right show how wolves stand in different ways, depending on their place in the order. You can see dogs doing this too.

Arctic wolves eat mainly caribou and young musk oxen. These pictures (seen from above) show a pack of wolves catching a caribou.

A pack of 4 wolves has spotted a mother caribou and her baby. The wolves line up, ready to start the chase.

The wolves move forward. Each takes a different path so the caribou are surrounded. The caribou panic and begin to run.

As the wolves move in closer, the baby caribou runs the wrong way and gets caught. The mother manages to escape.

Changing coats

Many Arctic animals have different coats in different seasons. In winter, their coats are white, so they are less easily seen against the snow. In summer, when the snow has melted, their coats are brown or grey, so they blend with rocks and plants.

Snowshoe hare in winter coat

Snowshoe hare in summer coat

Two kinds of hares live in the Arctic - snowshoe hares and Arctic hares. Hares can run very fast. They eat plants.

Stoat in winter coat

Stoat in summer coat

Stoats are very fierce. They eat birds and small mammals, such as lemmings (see below). The tip of a stoat's tail is always black. Stoats in their winter coats are called ermines.

Arctic fox in summer coat

Arctic fox in winter coat

Arctic foxes eat hares, stoats, birds and lemmings. They have smaller ears and less pointed noses than red foxes.

Lemmings

Norway lemming

Lemmings are small, plant-eating mammals. In winter, they live in burrows in the snow, sheltered from the cold and wind. They feed on plants which grow up through the soil. Lemmings are eaten by many other Arctic animals. When they are inside their burrows, they are out of sight, but some of their enemies still have ways of catching them.

Arctic foxes can sniff out lemmings in their burrows. This Arctic fox is rising up on its back paws, before crashing down, front paws first, through the snow on top of a burrow.

Stoats can fit down lemming burrows. They chase lemmings into their burrows and kill them by biting their necks.

Lemmings in snow burrow

Footprints in the snow

Different animals make different footprints in the snow. The line of footprints an animal leaves is called its trail. Here are the snow trails of three Arctic animals.

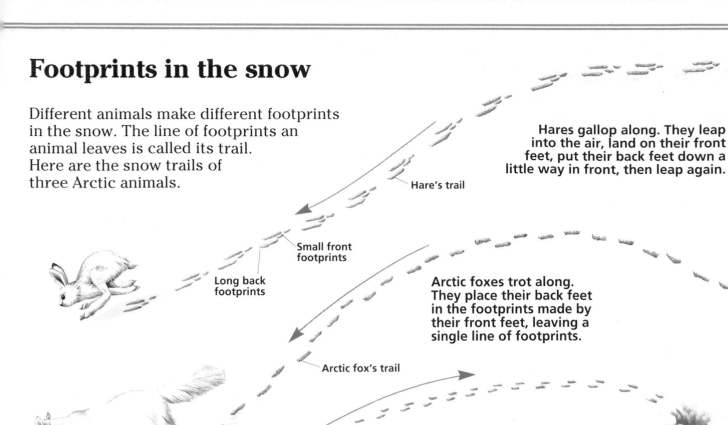

Hares gallop along. They leap into the air, land on their front feet, put their back feet down a little way in front, then leap again.

Hare's trail

Small front footprints

Long back footprints

Arctic foxes trot along. They place their back feet in the footprints made by their front feet, leaving a single line of footprints.

Arctic fox's trail

Stoat tunnelled into snow

Stoats jump along, leaving pairs of footprints. Every so often, they suddenly tunnel down into the snow to hunt small burrowing animals, such as lemmings.

Stoat comes out of tunnel

Stoat's trail

Lemming migrations

Lemmings give birth to up to eight babies every five weeks, so the number of lemmings in one area can grow very fast. When numbers get high, thousands of lemmings migrate to other areas, to find food. Many drown by running into rivers or lakes. These pictures show how the number of lemmings in an area can change over four years.

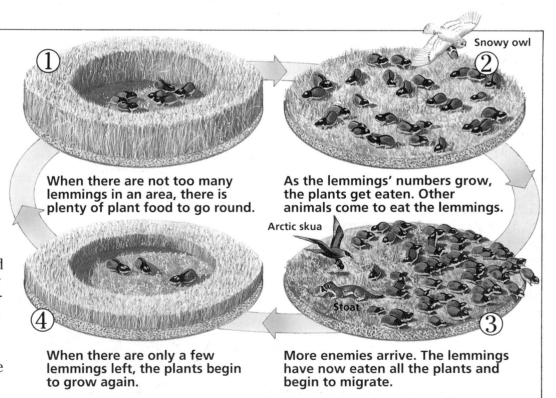

① ②

Snowy owl

When there are not too many lemmings in an area, there is plenty of plant food to go round.

As the lemmings' numbers grow, the plants get eaten. Other animals come to eat the lemmings.

Arctic skua

④ ③

Stoat

When there are only a few lemmings left, the plants begin to grow again.

More enemies arrive. The lemmings have now eaten all the plants and begin to migrate.

15

Whales

Whales are mammals which spend all their lives in the sea. There are nearly 80 different species. Many of the larger species swim long distances from one ocean to another. There are two main types of whales - baleen whales and toothed whales. They eat different sorts of food.

Baleen whales

Baleen whales eat krill (see page 6). Instead of teeth, they have fringes of tough skin, called baleen, which hang down inside their mouths. The two small pictures on the right show how most baleen whales feed.

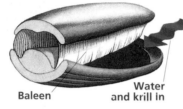

Whale's mouth open

Baleen

Water and krill in

Whale's mouth closed

Water out

The whale opens its mouth and takes a huge gulp of water. The water is full of krill.

When the whale closes its mouth, it sieves out the water through its baleen. The krill stays behind.

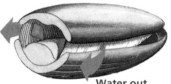

Minke whale

There are still a lot of minke whales in polar seas. Most other baleen whales have almost died out because of hunting.

Blue whales are the biggest animals that have ever lived. They weigh more than 30 elephants and their eyes are the size of soccer balls.

Blue whale

Callosities

Right whale

Humpback whale

Right whales have patches of tough, white skin, called callosities, on their heads. Scientists can recognize each right whale by the pattern of its callosities.

Humpback whales "talk" to each other by singing underwater. They make all kinds of whistling, rumbling and groaning noises.

Migration

Many baleen whales breed in winter in warm seas near the equator, and migrate to cold polar seas to feed during the summer. Some whales swim north to the Arctic and others swim south to the Antarctic. This map shows the migration routes of humpback whales.

Summer feeding places
Winter breeding places
→ Migration routes

Making a splash

Whales sometimes leap right out of the water and fall back in with a loud splash. This is called breaching. Nobody really knows why whales breach. It may be a way of communicating with other whales.

Humpback whale breaching

Blowing bubbles

Humpback whales sometimes make "nets" out of bubbles, to catch food. These pictures show how they do this.

The whale swims slowly to the surface in an upward spiral. As it swims, it blows air bubbles out of its blowhole.

The bubbles rise to the surface, making a circle. Krill collects in the middle of the circle.

With its mouth open, the whale bursts out of the water in the middle of the circle, and takes a huge gulp of krill.

Mothers and babies

These pictures show a mother right whale and her baby swimming along together. Baby whales are called calves.

Every now and then, the calf dives underneath its mother, so that it can feed on her milk.

When it has finished feeding, the calf makes its way back up to the surface, and carries on swimming.

Toothed whales

Toothed whales eat mainly fish and squid. They often live together in groups, called pods. Members of a pod "talk" to each other in whistles and clicks. Killer whales, sperm whales, belugas and narwhals are all toothed whales found in polar seas.

Beluga whales are very "chatty". They make all kinds of mooing, chirping, squeaking, whistling and clanging noises. Beluga whales live in the Arctic.

Beluga whale

Sperm whales helping an injured member of their pod

Narwhal

Members of a sperm whale pod often help each other. If one whale is injured, the others make a circle around it, supporting it near the surface so it can breathe.

Narwhals live in the Arctic. Males, and some females, have a spiral tusk, about 2m (7ft) long, which grows forward through their upper lip.

Whale tracking

Scientists track whales to find out more about their movements. The most modern way of tracking is by satellite. A radio transmitter is attached to a whale. As the whale swims along, the transmitter sends out signals which are picked up by a satellite going around the Earth. The satellite beams the information down to a receiving station on land.

Radio transmitter attached to beluga whale

This map shows how a beluga whale in the Arctic was tracked by a satellite. The whale was tracked for nearly 500km (311 miles) before its transmitter fell off.

Satellite picked up signal from radio transmitter each time it passed over whale.

Satellite beamed down information about whale's position each time it passed over receiving station.

Path of whale

Path of satellite

Radio transmitter on whale sent signals up to satellite

Tracking of whale started here

Receiving station on land

Killer whales

Killer whales are found in all seas, including polar seas. They are the fiercest whales. As well as fish and squid, they eat birds, seals and even other whales. They usually hunt in groups and share food with each other (see page 23).

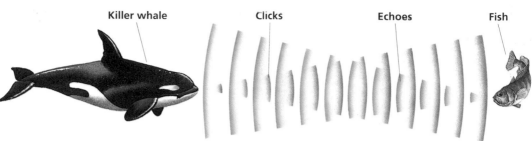

Killer whale   Clicks   Echoes   Fish

As they swim along, killer whales, and other toothed whales, make high-pitched clicking noises.

These clicks bounce off any object in their way, such as a fish, and send echoes back to the whale.

From these echoes, the whale can tell the position of the fish, and can catch it.

Blowing

Whales have to come to the surface of the sea to breathe. They blow out stale air and breathe in fresh air through a blowhole on the top of their heads. The air they blow out contains tiny drops of water, which spray upward. You can tell which species a whale is by the shape of its blow.

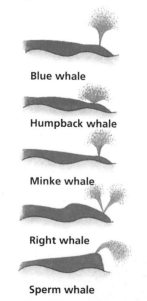

Blue whale

Humpback whale

Minke whale

Right whale

Sperm whale

Killer whales often hold themselves upright in the water, with their heads above the surface, to look around. This is called spy hopping.

19

Seals

Seals are mammals which live in the sea. In spring, they come on to land, or ice, to give birth to their babies, which are called pups. Seals are clumsy on land but are very good swimmers. They eat mainly fish, squid and krill. Seals are kept warm by their fur, and by a thick layer of fat under their skin. All the seals on these two pages live in the Arctic.

Harp seal pup

Mother harp seal

Harp seals are born with fluffy, white coats. Their mothers feed and take care of them for about 10 days. Then the pups grow their adult coats and must look after themselves.

Hooded seals

Hooded seals get their name because males can inflate the top part of their heads, into a kind of hood. They can also blow out the skin inside their noses, into a red balloon. They do this when they are excited or in danger.

Hooded seal with inflated hood

Hooded seal with inflated nostril

Hunting seals

The Inuit people who live in the Arctic have always hunted seals for food and to make clothes from their skins. Today, there are laws protecting seals from hunting, but Inuit who still depend on seals in order to survive are allowed to hunt a small number each year. You can find out more about hunting on page 31.

This Inuit hunter is waiting beside a hole in the ice for a seal to appear. His weapon is a traditional harpoon, but today many hunters use rifles instead.

Birth in a snow den

Ringed seals give birth to their pups in snow dens, to shelter them from the wind and to hide them from Arctic foxes and polar bears. They often make more than one den, so they can move the pup if there is danger.

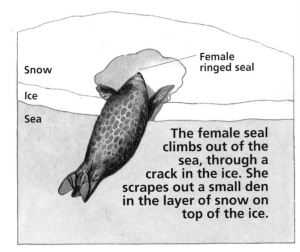

Snow

Ice

Sea

Female ringed seal

The female seal climbs out of the sea, through a crack in the ice. She scrapes out a small den in the layer of snow on top of the ice.

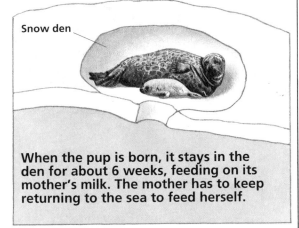

Snow den

When the pup is born, it stays in the den for about 6 weeks, feeding on its mother's milk. The mother has to keep returning to the sea to feed herself.

Arctic fox

If a fox or bear attacks and there is no time to move the pup, the mother slips back into the sea, leaving her pup behind.

Walruses

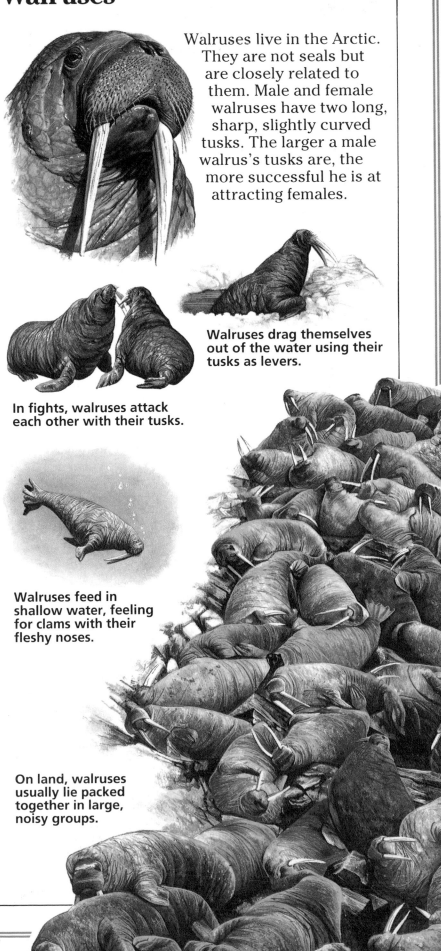

Walruses live in the Arctic. They are not seals but are closely related to them. Male and female walruses have two long, sharp, slightly curved tusks. The larger a male walrus's tusks are, the more successful he is at attracting females.

Walruses drag themselves out of the water using their tusks as levers.

In fights, walruses attack each other with their tusks.

Walruses feed in shallow water, feeling for clams with their fleshy noses.

On land, walruses usually lie packed together in large, noisy groups.

Eared seals and true seals

Eared seal

True seal

There are two main types of seals - those with ears (eared seals) and those without (true seals). Eared seals can turn their back flippers forward to help them waddle along on land. True seals cannot do this. They drag themselves along using their front flippers. Apart from Antarctic fur seals, all the seals in this book are true seals. The seals on these two pages live in the Antarctic.

Crabeater seals on ice floe

There are more crabeater seals than all the other seals in the world added together - over 15 million of them. In spite of their name, they eat krill, not crabs.

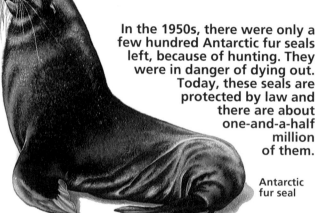

In the 1950s, there were only a few hundred Antarctic fur seals left, because of hunting. They were in danger of dying out. Today, these seals are protected by law and there are about one-and-a-half million of them.

Antarctic fur seal

Leopard seal's head

Leopard seals have huge heads and sharp, saw-like teeth. They are the only seals which eat other kinds of seals, but their main food is penguins (see page 11).

Living underwater

Seals are very well adapted to living underwater. Their bodies are a good shape and they have webbed flippers to help them swim. Weddell seals spend the whole winter in the sea, under the ice shelves around Antarctica. They have to come to the surface for air because, like whales, seals cannot breathe underwater.

Weddell seals make breathing holes in the ice, where they can come to the surface for air.

The seals keep their breathing holes open by scraping at the ice with their teeth.

Weddell seals can dive as deep as 800m (875yds) and stay underwater for an hour without coming up to breathe.

Weddell seal

Elephant seals

Elephant seals are the world's biggest seals. They get their name because the adult males have a loose, wrinkled piece of skin above their noses, which they can inflate into a kind of trunk. At breeding times, thousands of elephant seals gather in huge groups on beaches on islands around Antarctica. Pairs of males have long, fierce fights over females. The seal which is older and bigger usually wins.

Elephant seals fighting

When two elephant seals fight, they face each other, stretch their heads upward and roar loudly. Then they attack each other's necks with their teeth. They have thick skin on their necks to protect them.

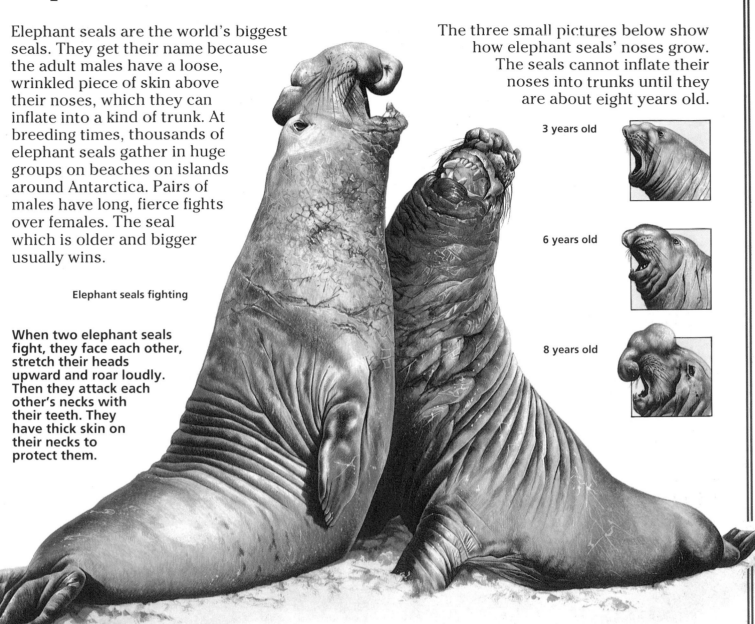

The three small pictures below show how elephant seals' noses grow. The seals cannot inflate their noses into trunks until they are about eight years old.

3 years old

6 years old

8 years old

Danger from killer whales

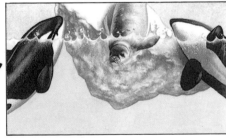

Killer whales eat all kinds of seals. Here, a group of killer whales has found a crabeater seal asleep on an ice floe. The whales move in and surround the floe.

One whale leans on the edge of the floe, using its weight to push the floe downward. Another whale pushes the floe upward from the other side. The seal begins to slip.

As the floe tilts, the seal slides off, straight into the jaws of one of the killer whales. The other whales will swim up to take their share of the food.

23

Arctic birds

Each spring, thousands of birds migrate to the Arctic, to feed and breed there during the summer. All kinds of food, such as plants and insects, are uncovered when the ice melts (see pages 28-29). In autumn, most birds leave to spend the winter in warmer places. Here are some of the birds that spend the summer in the Arctic.

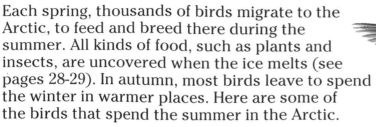

Fulmar

Arctic skua

Arctic redpoll

Snow bunting

Glaucous gull

Rough-legged buzzard

Turnstone

Golden plover

Red-necked phalarope

Gyrfalcon

Red-legged kittiwake

Little auk

Siberian white crane

Black-throated diver

Long-tailed duck

Harlequin duck

Barnacle goose

White-fronted goose

Snow goose

Brent goose

Bewick swan

Amazing Arctic terns

Arctic tern

Arctic terns fly further than any other birds. They travel from the Arctic to the Antarctic, and back again, every year - a distance of up to 40,000km (25,000 miles). When it is winter in the Arctic, they are in the Antarctic. When it is winter in the Antarctic, they are in the Arctic. So Arctic terns have two summers every year, and never have a winter.

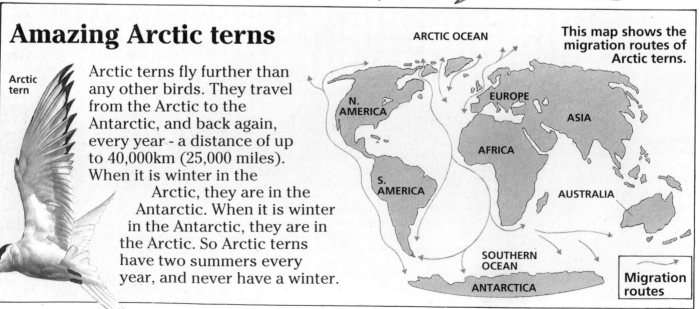

This map shows the migration routes of Arctic terns.

ARCTIC OCEAN

N. AMERICA

EUROPE

ASIA

AFRICA

S. AMERICA

AUSTRALIA

SOUTHERN OCEAN

ANTARCTICA

Migration routes

Staying for the winter

Snowy owls, ptarmigans and ravens stay on the Arctic tundra all through the winter. They have to survive the cold, find food for themselves and their chicks, and avoid being eaten by enemies, such as Arctic foxes.

Snowy owl with chicks

Snowy owls nest on the ground, usually on slightly raised areas, so they can keep a look-out for enemies. They do not lay all their eggs at once, so there may be chicks of different sizes in the nest. The adults bring lemmings for the chicks to feed on.

Ptarmigan in summer

Ptarmigans dig plants out of the snow with their feet. In winter, they are white, to blend with the snow. In summer, they are patchy brown, to blend with rocks and plants.

Ptarmigan in winter

Ravens are black all year long, so they do not blend with their background in summer or winter. They have few enemies, though, because they are so strong and fierce.

Raven

Nests on cliffs

Many Arctic birds lay their eggs on cliffs so enemies on the ground cannot reach them. They breed in large groups, called colonies. This picture shows some of the birds you might see nesting together on a cliff.

Puffins nest in burrows which they hollow out in the soil near the top of cliffs.

Puffins

Kittiwakes make messy nests on narrow cliff ledges.

Kittiwakes

Guillemots lay their eggs on bare ledges. The eggs are pointed at one end so that if they are knocked, they roll around in a circle, instead of forward off the ledge.

Guillemot egg

Guillemots

Razorbills lay their eggs on ledges under overhanging rocks.

Razorbills

Antarctic birds

Many types of birds live in the Antarctic as well as penguins. Penguins cannot fly, but most other Antarctic birds spend their lives flying over the stormy Southern Ocean, feeding on fish, squid and krill. They only come on to land to breed. The most common Antarctic birds are penguins, petrels and albatrosses.

Albatrosses

Albatrosses are the largest sea birds in the world. They also live longer than most other birds - it is quite common for albatrosses to live for 30 years and some live for 70 or 80 years. Four species of albatrosses breed in the Antarctic. They usually breed in large colonies, with thousands of nests together.

Wandering albatross

Wandering albatrosses can travel as far as 3,750km (2,330 miles) in one day. They use their long, narrow wings to glide along on air currents.

Wandering albatrosses have longer wings than any other bird. The distance from the tip of one wing to the tip of the other can be as much as 3.5m (11.5ft). This means each wing is about the length of a person.

Grey-headed albatross chick on nest

Albatrosses make raised nests out of mud, grass and moss. They hollow out the top, line it with grass and feathers and lay a single egg inside. When the chick hatches, it sits on top of the nest.

Finding a partner

Albatrosses take a long time to find a partner, but it is something that most of them only have to do once. Pairs of albatrosses usually stay together for their whole lives. These pictures show how a pair gets together.

The male attracts females by doing a courtship display. He points his beak upward, holds out his wings and whistles.

When a female arrives, the two dance face to face. They stretch out their wings and snap their beaks loudly.

When they have paired up, the birds sit side by side on the nest area, nibbling at each other's necks and calling softly.

26

Diving for fish

Blue-eyed shags swim along on the surface of the sea and dive to the bottom to catch fish.

They swim back up to the surface with the fish, eat it and then dive again immediately.

After 2 or 3 dives, they often stand on a rock and hold their wings out to dry.

Petrels

Petrels are related to albatrosses. There are 18 different species living in the Antarctic. Here are three of them.

Snow petrels hover over the pack ice around Antarctica. They dive down between the ice floes to snatch krill out of the water.

Snow petrel

Giant petrels are the largest petrels. They have enormous beaks which look as if they are made up of lots of pieces.

Storm petrels flutter along just above the surface of the sea, with their legs dangling down. They look as if they are walking on the water.

Wilson's storm petrel

Giant petrel

Chick snatchers

Large, fierce birds, called skuas, sometimes snatch and eat the chicks of other birds, such as penguins. They wait around near penguin rookeries until they see a chick which has wandered away from the crèche. Then they rush in and snatch it. Skuas also steal penguin eggs which have been left unguarded.

This gentoo penguin is trying to stop a skua from snatching her chick.

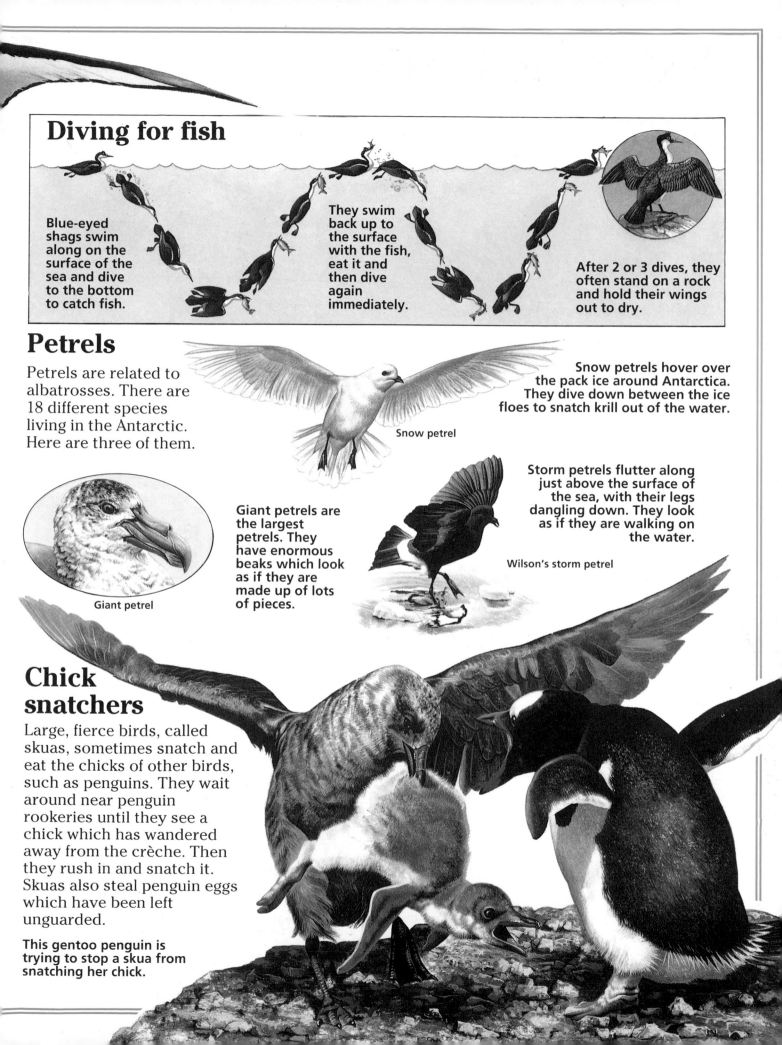

Summer in the Arctic

During summer in the Arctic, some of the ice on the tundra melts. Plants grow, insects hatch and lemmings come out of their burrows. This means there is suddenly plenty of food, both for animals which have spent all winter on the tundra, and for those which arrive just for the summer. They can even feed all night because in the Arctic the sun never sets in summer. The summer is short, though - after six to eight weeks, the ground freezes and winter begins again.

Mosses and lichens are the most common Arctic plants. Lichens grow very slowly and may take hundreds of years to grow 3cm (about an inch).

Lichens

Mosses

Flowering plants

It is hard for plants to grow in the Arctic. Even in summer, it is cold and windy. In winter, there is no sunshine and all the water is frozen into ice. When the ice does melt, the soil is often flooded. Despite all this, over a thousand species of flowering plants grow on the tundra. Here are some of them.

Arctic poppy

Moss campion

Campanulas

Purple saxifrage

Yellow avens

Buttercups

Diapensia

Yellow mountain saxifrage

Arctic azalea

Flocks of birds arrive to feed on plants and insects, and to raise their chicks. The chicks have to grow quickly so they can fly back to warmer places before the Arctic winter begins.

Flock of snow geese

Arctic poppies

Purple saxifrage

Cotton grass

In summer, caribou and other mammals are pestered by biting insects, such as mosquitoes and blackflies. Millions of insects hatch out of their eggs which have been frozen in ponds and lakes all winter.

Tundra food web

This food web shows who eats what on the Arctic tundra. For example, lemmings eat plants, and are eaten by skuas, snowy owls, Arctic foxes and stoats. (The pictures are not to scale.)

Arctic foxes

Wolves

Skuas

Snowy owls

Stoats

Hares

Musk oxen

Caribou

Lemmings

Ptarmigans

Plants

Boggy tundra

The ice on the surface of the tundra melts in summer, but about 1m (3ft) below is a thick layer of ice, called permafrost, which never melts. Water cannot drain through the permafrost, so it stays on the tundra, in bogs and ponds.

Permafrost

Chilly Antarctic

Antarctica is much colder than the Arctic tundra. Even in summer, most of the land is covered with ice. On the outer edges of Antarctica, there are mosses, lichens, two species of flowering plants and a few insects.

People in polar lands

People, such as the Inuit and the Sami, have been living in the Arctic for thousands of years, without harming their environment. When outsiders came to the Arctic, and later to the Antarctic, they were not so careful, as you can find out on page 31.

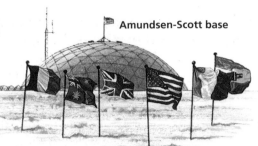
Amundsen-Scott base

Nobody lives in the Antarctic, but scientists from many countries spend time there, learning about the place and its wildlife. The US scientific base near the South Pole is called Amundsen-Scott.

The Inuit

Arctic hare carved out of walrus tusk

The Inuit live in North America and Greenland. In the past, they moved around in small family groups, living in ice houses, called igloos. They survived by fishing and hunting. Hunters often carved things out of the tusks and bones of the animals that they killed. Today, many Inuit stay in one place instead of moving around. They live in houses in towns and go to work every day.

Inuit still build igloos to spend the night in when they go on hunting trips. Igloos are made from blocks of ice. The cracks are filled in with loose snow.

The Sami

Sami tent made from reindeer skins

The Sami people of Scandinavia and Russia used to survive by keeping herds of reindeer. They got meat and milk from them, and used their skins to make clothes, and tents to live in. They also used the reindeer to carry loads and to pull sledges. Some Sami still live in this way today, but, like the Inuit, many have given up their old way of life and now live and work in towns instead.

This brightly dressed Sami woman is a reindeer-herder. Many herders travel along the reindeer migration routes, stopping whenever the reindeer stop to feed.

Polar explorers

In 1909, Robert Peary became the first person to reach the North Pole. The first person to reach the South Pole was Roald Amundsen. He got there on 14th December 1911, beating another explorer, Robert Falcon Scott, by just 35 days. Scott and all his companions died on their way back.

Explorers struggled across the ice in freezing temperatures and bitter winds. Teams of dogs pulled sledges piled with food and equipment.

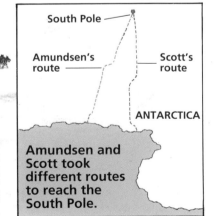
South Pole

Amundsen's route

Scott's route

ANTARCTICA

Amundsen and Scott took different routes to reach the South Pole.

Hunting

Outsiders did not hunt for their own survival, but sold huge numbers of animal skins for money. Polar bears, musk oxen and many species of seals and whales almost died out in some areas. Today, most species are protected.

In the Canadian Arctic, thousands of baby harp seals used to be killed every year for their fur. Today, very few are killed because fewer people want to wear fur coats.

Fishing

Since the 1970s, people have been catching large amounts of fish, squid and krill. If numbers of these get too low, the animals which eat them, such as seals and whales, will suffer too. This can be stopped if people agree to limit how much they catch.

Modern fishing boats can catch huge amounts at one time. Animals, such as sea birds and seals, can get caught in the nets by mistake.

Pollution

Polar areas are not as polluted as other places, because they are far away from big groups of people. In the Arctic, though, oil pollution is a problem. For example, in 1989, off the coast of Alaska, USA, a lot of oil spilled into the sea from the Exxon Valdez tanker. In cold water, oil takes years to break up and disappear.

If sea birds swallow oil, they are poisoned. They can also die of cold if oil clogs their feathers.

The ozone layer

In the Earth's atmosphere, a layer of gas, called ozone, protects plants and animals from the sun's harmful rays. In 1982, scientists discovered that the ozone layer above Antarctica was very thin. They believe it is being destroyed by gases, called CFCs, which come from things such as refrigerators and aerosols.

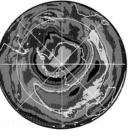

This satellite picture shows the thinning, or "hole", in the ozone layer above Antarctica. The hole is the orange part in the middle.

Building

In the Arctic, people mine for oil, coal, and so on. Mining, fishing and hunting lead to the building of roads, mines, ports, pipelines and airstrips (places for planes to land). This changes the environment and can disturb wildlife.

In Antarctica, penguins' breeding areas have been dug up to build airstrips. The environmental group, Greenpeace, has been trying to stop this from happening.

Peace for polar lands

So far, 40 countries have agreed to protect Antarctica. In 1991, they decided that no mining would be allowed for 50 years. Conservation groups also work to protect polar lands. The Arctic and the Antarctic have not yet been spoiled like so many other places. It is not too late to keep them like this, so plants, animals and people can go on living there in peace.

Tourists can only visit Antarctica on carefully organized trips, so animals, such as these albatrosses, are not disturbed too much.

31

RAINFOREST WILDLIFE

Antonia Cunningham

Scientific consultants: Mark Collins and Gill Standring

Contents

Inside the rainforest

Rainforests are some of the oldest and most amazing wild places in the world. They are home to millions of different kinds, or species, of plants and animals. Inside a rainforest, it is always hot, dark and damp. Enormous trees tower about 30m (100ft) above the forest floor, forming a sort of roof which blocks out most of the sunshine. The canopy is so thick that rain can take ten minutes to reach the ground. The main picture shows part of a rainforest in Southeast Asia.

Trees called emergents tower above the canopy.

Canopy

This area between the canopy and the floor is called the understory.

Floor

Macaques

Each part of the forest is home to different animals and plants. Many animals do not travel far. The area that they move around in is called their territory or home range.

Habitats and food webs

The type of place where an animal lives is called its habitat. In each habitat there are different types of food. Plants get food from the soil and can make food using sunlight. Animals eat plants or other animals. The way that animals and plants are connected through the food they eat is called a food web. This picture shows part of a food web in a South American rainforest.

The arrows point from the plant or animal that is eaten to the animal that eats it.

Eagle

Jaguar

Monkey

Humming-bird

Caiman

Sloth

Capybara

Tamandua

Insect

Fish

Tapir

Flowers

Water plants

Termite

Leaves

Fruit

Seeds

Wood

Leaves, fruit, dead animals and droppings rot in the soil to form food for plants.

Porcupine

Gibbon

Orchids

Tree snake

Rainforest trees never lose all their leaves at once. They are always green. The leaves of different trees never touch.

Dusky leaf monkey

Over half the furry animals in the forest live in the canopy. It is also home to many birds, snakes and frogs.

Big roots called buttress roots grow down from the trunks of the tallest trees. They help to keep the tree upright.

Vines called lianas

Giant squirrel

Pentail tree shrew

Rafflesia

Leopard cat

Fruit on different trees ripens at different times. Many animals come to eat ripe fruit.

Many rainforest animals hunt, kill and eat other animals. Animals which hunt are called predators. Animals which are killed are called prey.

Mouse deer

35

Rainforests of the world

Rainforests grow in an area around the middle of the Earth called the tropics where it is always hot and rainy. In most rainforests, it rains nearly every day and the temperature in the day is usually about 30°C (86°F). These hot, wet forests are called tropical rainforests. The map below shows where the world's tropical rainforests grow.

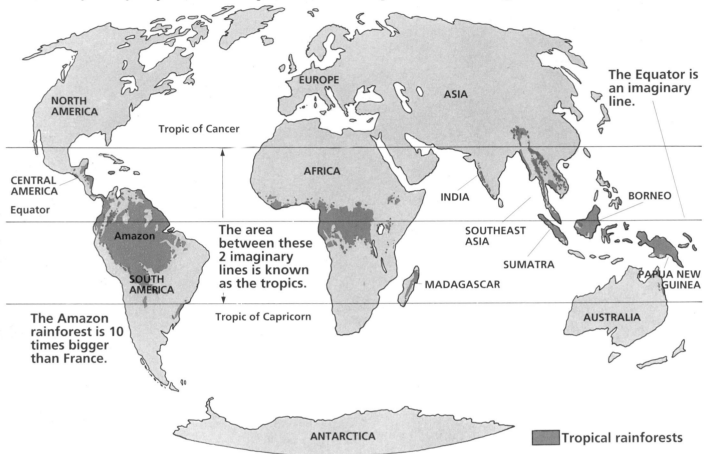

The Equator is an imaginary line.

EUROPE

ASIA

NORTH AMERICA

Tropic of Cancer

CENTRAL AMERICA

Equator

AFRICA

INDIA

BORNEO

Amazon

The area between these 2 imaginary lines is known as the tropics.

SOUTHEAST ASIA

SUMATRA

SOUTH AMERICA

MADAGASCAR

PAPUA NEW GUINEA

The Amazon rainforest is 10 times bigger than France.

Tropic of Capricorn

AUSTRALIA

ANTARCTICA

Tropical rainforests

Forests in danger

Rainforests are in danger because they are being cut down for wood, or to clear land for farming. This means that thousands of plants and animals lose their homes. Many countries have cut down so much rainforest that there is hardly any left. You can find out what people are doing to save rainforests and rainforest animals on pages 62-63.

AFRICA

This is the area shown on the big map on the right.

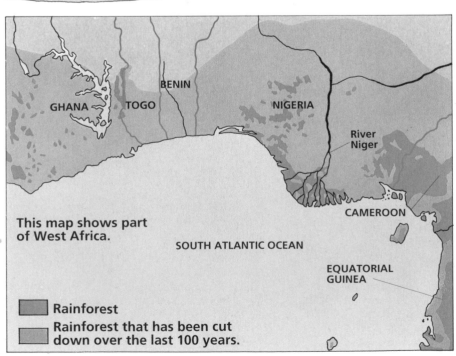

BENIN

GHANA

TOGO

NIGERIA

River Niger

This map shows part of West Africa.

SOUTH ATLANTIC OCEAN

CAMEROON

EQUATORIAL GUINEA

Rainforest

Rainforest that has been cut down over the last 100 years.

Rainforest plants and animals

Every rainforest in the world is different. Many species of animals and plants only live in rainforests in one area. Some scientists think that millions of years ago, all the land on Earth was joined together in one piece. They call this land Pangaea. They think that Pangaea split up over millions of years and that the pieces moved away from each other. This separated the animals and the plants too. Then, over millions of years, the plants and animals changed to suit their habitats. This change is known as adaptation.

200 million years ago

100 million years ago

50 million years ago

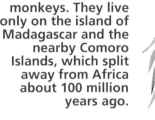

Ruffed lemur

Lemurs are related to monkeys. They live only on the island of Madagascar and the nearby Comoro Islands, which split away from Africa about 100 million years ago.

Marsupials carry their babies in pouches. They live in South America, Papua New Guinea and Australia, which were all once joined to Antarctica. Nearby islands, which split off from Asia, have no marsupials.

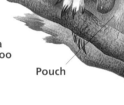

New Guinea tree kangaroo

Pouch

Rainforests and the weather

Trees help make rain. If they are cut down, it rains less.

1. Trees soak up water through their roots. It goes up into the leaves and branches.

If trees are cut down, rain can cause very bad floods.

2. Water from the leaves goes into the air all the time. When the sun warms them, this happens faster.

4. When the clouds are too heavy, the water falls as rain.

3. The water in the air joins together to form clouds.

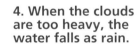

Rain trickles through the trees before reaching the ground. Tree roots hold the soil together and soak up water.

When there are no trees, the rain beats down hard, washing away the top layers of soil, which plants need so they can grow.

The soil washes into nearby rivers. Some is washed far away. The soil builds up in rivers and mud banks are formed.

Extra soil in the rivers means there is less room for water. If it rains hard, the rivers overflow, causing bad floods.

Apes and monkeys

Most of the world's monkeys and apes live in rainforests, feeding mainly on fruit and leaves. Monkeys are not apes. They are usually smaller and spend more of their time leaping around in the canopy. They have special thumbs which help them grasp branches easily and long tails which help them balance. Monkeys live all over the world, including Asia, South America and Africa. The four types of apes - gorillas, chimpanzees, gibbons and orangutans - have no tails. Gorillas and chimps live in Africa, orangutans and gibbons live in Southeast Asia.

Red uakari

South American monkeys have flat noses and wide nostrils.

Red colobus monkey

Monkeys from Southeast Asia and Africa have narrow noses.

Skeletons

Skeletons help show how animals move. Monkeys have thin hips and long backs, suited to climbing and leaping. Apes have long arms, suited to swinging in trees. Humans have long legs and can walk upright.

Spider monkey

Orangutan

Gorilla

Human

Gorillas

Gorillas are the largest type of ape. They are very intelligent, peaceful animals. They live in family groups made up of several females and their young, led by a large, adult male. Adult males are called silverbacks because the fur on their backs is silver. Gorillas mainly stay on the ground and spend most mornings and afternoons eating. They rest at midday. At night they sleep in nests made of leaves and broken branches, which are usually raised off the floor of the forest.

Gorillas are vegetarians. They eat leaves and plant stems.

AFRICA

Gorillas live in some parts of Africa. The rarest are mountain gorillas. Only about 600 are left in the wild.

Areas where gorillas live

Young adult males leave their family group when they are about 11 to 13 years old. They join or form new families.

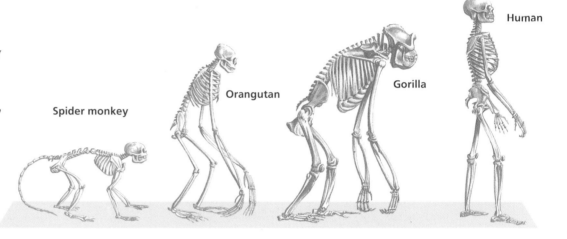

Young adult male

Moving through the trees

Brachiating gibbon

Prehensile tails are very strong.

Black-handed spider monkey

Apes and monkeys move through the forest in many ways. Gibbons have long arms and swing between trees, hand over hand, under the branches. This is called brachiating. They can leap distances of up to 15m (50ft). Some South American monkeys have tails called prehensile tails, which they use as extra arms to hang from trees. The ends are very sensitive. Spider monkeys can even use them to pick up nuts.

Silverback

These gorillas are grooming each other.

Female gorillas

Grooming shows that gorillas feel friendly toward each other. Females sometimes groom each other, and often groom their babies and the silverback.

Male gorillas can grow to about 1.7m (5ft 8in) tall. When their arms are spread out they are almost twice as wide as they are tall. In the wild they can live to be about 35 years old.

Young gorillas often play with each other or with the silverback. These gorillas are playing follow the leader.

Females are smaller than males. They grow up to 1.5m (5ft) tall. Baby gorillas start crawling when they are about 9 weeks old and walk after 30 to 40 weeks.

Orangutans

Orangutan means "person of the forest". An adult orangutan is about half as tall as an adult human. Orangutans usually live alone, but babies live with their mothers. Like other apes, females only give birth to one baby at a time. Orangutans rarely come down to the ground. At night, they sleep high up, in nests made out of leaves and broken branches. They mainly eat fruit, leaves and plant shoots. They drink rainwater from holes in trees. They live in Southeast Asia on the islands of Borneo and Sumatra.

Orangutans move through the trees by reaching out and grabbing the next branch or next liana along. They can stretch between branches over 2m (6½ft) apart, which is over twice their own height.

Adult males have long, dark faces with fatty lumps on each side. In Sumatra they also have beards.

Female orangutan

A baby orangutan clings to its mother's body.

Liana

A female orangutan has a baby every 3 to 6 years. A baby rides on its mother's body and sleeps in the same nest until the mother has another baby.

Amazing monkeys

Monkeys can "talk" to each other in many ways. From far away they call to keep in contact with their group and to warn strangers away. Face and body movements can signal feelings. Even skin can show if a monkey is male or female and how important it is in its own group.

Mandrills have very bright faces and bottoms. Adult males have the most vivid skin. It becomes brighter than usual when they are angry or excited.

Mandrill

Howler monkeys get their name from their very loud calls which can be heard over long distances. Groups of howler monkeys call to each other early each morning.

Black howler monkey

Male proboscis monkeys have noses up to 18cm (7in) long. These help them make loud honking noises when they are scared or want to call their group together.

Proboscis monkey

Chimpanzees

There are two types of chimpanzees - common chimps and pygmy chimps. They both live in rainforests in Africa. Chimps mostly eat plants and insects, but some chimps in West Africa have been found which often hunt and eat colobus monkeys.

Termite mound

This chimp is unhappy because he is not getting what he wants.

Monkeys and apes usually show their teeth when they are angry.

Chimps make and use tools. They put nuts or hard-skinned fruit on flat stones and smash them open with rocks.

Chimps poke sticks into termite mounds to catch termites. The termites cover the stick and the chimps eat them.

Before a hunt, chimps drum on tree roots and hoot to call each other. Then, silently, they wander along the forest floor, searching for monkeys in the canopy.

When they see some monkeys, one chimp, who is known as the driver, rushes up a tree and tries to separate one or two monkeys from the main group.

If a monkey is cut off, several chimps, known as blockers, dash into the trees and sit on branches on each side of the monkey's escape route. Other chimps chase it.

The oldest chimp has to guess in advance where the monkey will run. He goes to this place and blocks its escape. The chasers catch the monkey and kill it.

Monkey food

Most monkeys eat leaves and fruit, but some are adapted to eat more unusual things.

Saki

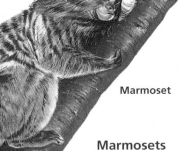

Marmoset

Long-tailed macaque

Sakis place hard seeds in a special gap between their teeth, which makes it easier to crack the seeds open.

Marmosets are the only monkeys that eat gum and sap. They have special teeth which help them gnaw holes in tree trunks to let the gum drip out.

Long-tailed macaques from Southeast Asia live near rivers. They search the mud by the river's edge for crabs, snails and other small animals. They are very good swimmers and often go into the water.

41

The rainforest at night

Rainforests are as busy at night as in the day. When daytime animals go to sleep, many others wake up. These are called nocturnal animals. They call to each other in the darkness. Frogs croak, night monkeys hoot, bushbabies chirp. Nocturnal animals live at all levels in forests all over the world. Deer, okapi, armadillos and agoutis look for food on the ground. Tarsiers, bushbabies and night monkeys live in the canopy and in the understory. Bats flit through the trees. Insects, such as fireflies, signal to each other with bright flashes of light. Even some flowers open up especially at night.

Night monkeys

Bush baby

Armadillo

Night eyes

Eyes need light to work. Light enters a hole in the eye called the pupil. At night there is very little light, so nocturnal animals need big eyes and pupils which let in as much light as possible.

The size of the pupil changes, depending on how much light there is. When there is too much light, the pupils become smaller so the insides of the eyes do not become damaged.

Tarsiers from Southeast Asia have huge eyes. One eye can weigh as much as their whole brain.

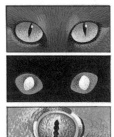

Cat's eye in bright light

Cat's eye in dim light

Gecko's eye in bright light

Gecko's eye in dim light

Fishing cat

Nocturnal animals have a special layer at the back of their eyes which helps them see at night. It makes their eyes glow in the dark if they are caught in a bright light.

Night life

Scientists do not know exactly why some animals are nocturnal but think that they may prefer the cooler temperature. Night may also be a good time to find food, as fewer animals are feeding. It is also easier to escape from predators in the dark. Some animals do not see well at night, but signal to each other or find food in other ways.

In the mangrove swamps of Southeast Asia, fireflies light up whole trees, flashing on and off together to signal for mates.

Flashing tail

New Guinea tree frog

Throat sac

Frogs croak to call to other frogs. Some have large throat sacs which they fill with air to help them call more loudly.

Pit viper

Pit organ

Pit vipers have little holes in their heads, called pit organs, which can sense the heat other animals give out. This means they can track their prey in the dark.

Bats

There are nearly a thousand different species of bats in the world. Different bats eat fruit, insects, small animals, or a sweet liquid from flowers, called nectar. Many bats live in rainforests. The biggest are Malay fruit bats (also called flying foxes), which live in Southeast Asia. During the day, thousands of fruit bats hang upside-down by their claws in the tops of trees or in caves. At night they may fly as far as 70km (over 40 miles) to find food.

1st finger

2nd finger

Thumb

3rd finger

4th finger

Malay fruit bat

When its wings are open, a Malay fruit bat is over 1.3m (4ft 2in) wide - about as wide as you are, when you hold your arms out.

Head looks like a fox's head.

Bat wings have fingers, thumbs and claws. The claws can grip firmly when the bat is hanging upside-down.

Kitti's hog-nosed bat

Claws are curved and sharp.

Kitti's hog-nosed bats are the world's smallest bats. They weigh 1.5g (0.05oz) and are only 15cm (6in) wide with their wings open. You can hold one in the palm of your hand.

Finding food

Bats find food in different ways. Some, such as fruit bats, can see and smell their food. Fringe-lipped bats find frogs to eat by listening for the frogs' mating calls. Other bats track insects by using a method called echo-location, which is shown in these pictures.

Bats let out high-pitched squeaks as they fly. The sounds bounce off objects, and back to the bats as echoes.

Bats know from the echoes if the object is an insect. They track an insect by following the changing direction of the echoes.

They grab their prey in their mouths and eat it as they fly. Some insects can hear bat squeaks and avoid being caught.

Gliders

Some animals can glide from tree to tree instead of leaping. This is a good way to travel long distances and escape most predators. However, gliders are still easy targets for hungry birds. To lessen the danger, many of them are patterned to blend in with their surroundings. Most of them only come out at night when it is harder for predators to spot them.

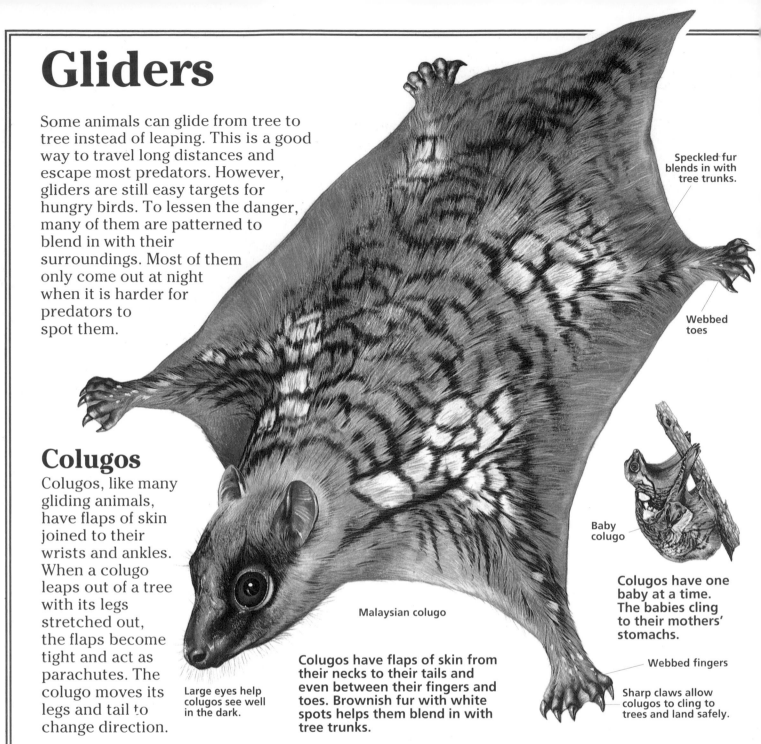

Speckled fur blends in with tree trunks.

Webbed toes

Baby colugo

Colugos have one baby at a time. The babies cling to their mothers' stomachs.

Webbed fingers

Sharp claws allow colugos to cling to trees and land safely.

Malaysian colugo

Colugos

Colugos, like many gliding animals, have flaps of skin joined to their wrists and ankles. When a colugo leaps out of a tree with its legs stretched out, the flaps become tight and act as parachutes. The colugo moves its legs and tail to change direction.

Large eyes help colugos see well in the dark.

Colugos have flaps of skin from their necks to their tails and even between their fingers and toes. Brownish fur with white spots helps them blend in with tree trunks.

Flying squirrels

Flying squirrels sleep in the day in tree holes. In Indonesia and Malaysia some make nests in coconut shells. At dusk, they climb into the tree tops to feed on leaves, plant shoots and nuts.

Flying squirrels launch themselves into the air, with their front and back legs stretched out.

They can glide as far as 100m (328ft) between trees. They often travel long distances to find food.

When they land, they turn around to face downward, ready to rush to safety in a tree hole if necessary.

Lizards, snakes and frogs

When a lizard is feeding or resting, its flaps are folded away against its body.

Flying lizards are some of the most common gliders in Southeast Asian rainforests. They are about 15cm (6in) long and have flying flaps joined to their ribs. To fly, they pull their ribs out, making a stiff flap on each side. Then they leap into the air. They can glide up to 15m (50ft) between trees and can change position and roll over while in the air.

Three species of tree snakes can glide. They do not have flying flaps. Instead, they raise their rib-cages upward and outward. This flattens out their bodies which then act like parachutes. With S-shaped movements from side to side, a snake can glide as far as 50m (165ft).

Flying lizard

Ribs

Ornate flying snake

Flying snake's ribs when resting

Flying snake's ribs when flying

Flying fish

Freshwater hatchet fish in the Amazon River can glide in the air up to 10m (33ft) scientist think they may even really fly, flapping their fins.

South American gliding tree frog

Webs

Several tree frogs glide. They have long, widely-spaced toes with webs between them. These help them glide in the way that flying flaps do. Gliding frogs use their legs to steer to the left or right as they glide. They can cover gaps up to 12m (40ft) wide.

Plants

Half of all plant species grow in rainforests. Many different kinds of plants can grow in a very small area. In Costa Rica, for example, scientists discovered 233 species in an area about a tenth of the size of a soccer field.

Orchids

There are over 35,000 species of orchids in the world. More than three-quarters of them grow in rainforests.

Finding food and water

Rainforest plants grow down near the forest floor, high in the trees, and even on other plants. They get some food from the soil but they also make their own food from sunlight which they take in through their leaves. Different plants can survive on different amounts of light. Plants that need lots of light grow high up in the trees and their roots take in water from the air. Plants that survive on less light live nearer the ground.

Bromeliads mostly grow in the canopy. They fill with rainwater and many small animals live in the water, trapped between their leaves. Some bromeliads can hold up to 54 litres (12 gallons) of water.

Bromeliad

Leaves up in the canopy take in a great deal of sunlight.

Many orchids grow in the canopy.

Orchid

Moss

Roots

Liana

Woody vines called lianas climb into the tree tops to reach the sun. They often stretch between trees and hang in thick loops.

Many leaves have pointed ends called drip tips. When it rains, the rain runs off the drip tip. This helps the leaf dry quickly and stops moss from growing on it and blocking out the light.

Drip tip

Pitcher plants

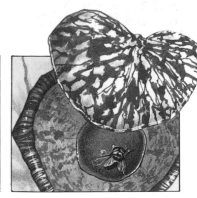

Pitcher plants catch insects. They have jug-shaped leaves which are about half full of a special liquid.

Insects are attracted by the way the plant smells and looks. They land on the rim of the jug, looking for food.

The rim of the jug is waxy and the insects slip and fall into the liquid. They cannot climb up the sides to get out again.

The liquid makes the insects dissolve (like salt in hot water). The plant takes in the dissolved insects as food.

Attracting animals

Plants often need animals, such as insects, birds and bats to help them spread seeds. The animals help do this when they fly from flower to flower, feeding on nectar, a sweet liquid food. When an animal puts its head inside a flower to sip the nectar, it becomes covered in a golden dust called pollen. When it feeds on another flower, the pollen rubs off. If the flowers belong to the same species, the pollen will make the second plant grow seeds. Animals are usually only attracted to certain flowers. This makes them more likely to carry pollen between flowers of the same species.

Scarlet honey-eater

Most birds cannot smell, but can see very well. Flowers which mainly attract birds are very bright, often orange or red. They do not often have a strong smell.

Banana Flower

Some bats can smell and see well. Flowers which attract them smell damp and only open at night. The bats can see them in the dark because most are quite pale.

Flying fox

Orchid

Carpenter bee

Some flowers have a special smell which attracts only one type of insect. One species of orchid attracts only male carpenter bees because they smell like female carpenter bees.

Jungle giants

The hot, wet weather in rainforests helps many plants grow to huge sizes.

Rafflesia plants have the world's biggest flowers. They are 1m (3ft) across and weigh 6kg (13lbs). Rafflesias smell of rotting meat. This attracts insects that feed on the bodies of dead animals.

Rafflesia flower

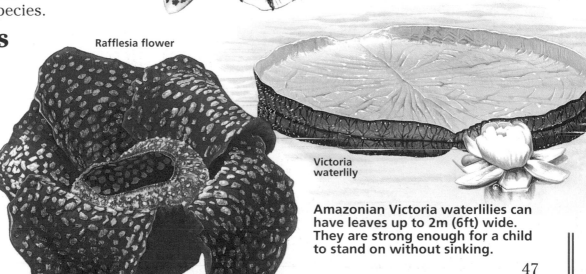

Victoria waterlily

Amazonian Victoria waterlilies can have leaves up to 2m (6ft) wide. They are strong enough for a child to stand on without sinking.

Birds of the rainforest

There are over 9,000 species of birds in the world. Over 2,500 of them live in rainforests and 1,700 species live only in South America. Birds are very important in forests because they drop seeds which grow into new plants. They have many different living and feeding habits.

Philippine eagle

Hooked beak

Sharp claws

Birds of prey, such as rare Philippine eagles, eat meat. They fly fast and have sharp claws to grab and kill animals, and a hooked beak to rip them apart. They can see animals from a great distance.

Violet-cheeked hummingbird

Hummingbirds are named after the sound their wings make when they fly. To eat, they poke their beaks into flowers and suck up the nectar through their tube-like tongues. Hummingbirds can fly on the spot, by moving their wings backward and forward in the shape of an eight, up to 3,000 times a minute. They are also the only birds that can fly backward.

Red-capped parrot

Parrots are very common in rainforests. They feed in groups on seeds and nuts. They use their feet to hold food.

Wings move in the shape of an eight.

Keel-billed toucan

Toucans live in South America. They have large, light bills and long tongues. They feed on fruit, spiders and insects. Toucans make nests in tree holes and both of the parents look after the young.

Winter travel

Many birds which live in cool parts of the world fly south to rainforests in the winter to escape the cold of their own countries. They fly back to breed in summer.

North America

Yellow warbler

South America

Flight of the yellow warbler

48

Finding a mate

Birds have many ways of attracting a mate. Some male birds have bright feathers which they display to females. Others sing, or do a kind of dance called a courtship display. Sometimes a male and female do a courtship display together.

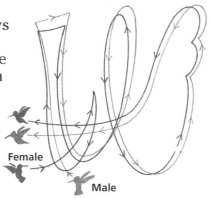

Female

Male

Male and female hummingbirds do a courtship dance together.

Female

Bower

Male

Male satin bowerbirds from Papua New Guinea make structures, called bowers, from twigs and grasses, to attract females. They decorate them with mud and bright objects such as bluebird feathers.

This shows the courtship display of the male Raggiana bird of paradise.

Extraordinary birds

Many extraordinary birds live in rainforests around the world. Here are some of them.

Hoatzin

Hoatzins smell like cow dung. This is because they eat leaves and as the leaves rot in their stomachs, they give off a bad smell.

Baby hoatzins have claws which they use to climb trees.

Baby hoatzin

Claws

Quetzal

Central American quetzals spread avocado seeds. They swallow small avocados and later throw the seeds back up from their stomachs.

Golden cock-of-the-rock

Golden cocks-of-the-rock live in South America, near the forest floor. They eat fruit and insects.

Casque

Tarictic hornbills

There are 45 species of hornbills. They have a lump on their beaks called a casque. Males have bigger casques than females. Casques may be used to attract a mate. Female hornbills lay their eggs inside trees. They block the entrance and the male feeds them through a tiny hole.

49

Wild cats

Over three-quarters of all types of wild cats live in forests. Most of these live in rainforests. Cats vary in size but they are all meat eaters, have excellent eyesight, can run very fast and are good tree climbers. Most of them are also nocturnal. Big cats can roar but small cats can only purr and meow. Most cats usually live and hunt alone. They mark out their territory, or home range, by leaving smells or claw marks on trees and rocks which warn other cats to stay away. The cats on these pages all live in rainforests, but many of them can also live in other types of forest, or on open grassland.

Jaguars

Jaguars are the only big cats that live in Central and South America. They are very good swimmers and like living in thick forest, near water. They mainly eat animals such as peccaries, capybaras and fish. They sometimes even catch and eat crocodiles.

Every jaguar has a different pattern of whiskers and coat markings in the same way as every human has a different set of finger prints.

At birth, jaguars are less than 40cm (16in) long. They are born with their eyes shut. These open up after about 13 days.

Some jaguars are born with black fur. They are not a different species of jaguar.

In the dark, jaguars and other big cats can see about 6 times better than humans. They have very strong jaws and teeth which can bite through bones very easily.

Cubs stay with their mothers for about 2 years. They can have babies themselves when they are about 3 years old.

Coat markings

Wild cats usually have yellow or brownish fur with spotted or striped markings. At night, or in the patchy daylight of the forest, this helps them blend in with the light and shade of their surroundings. This makes it easier for them to hide when they are hunting.

Because most animals can only see in black and white, this is what a clouded leopard in a tree would look like to them. Notice how the its patterned markings help break up the outline of its body against its background.

Clouded leopard

Tigers

Tigers are the largest cats. They are very strong and can catch big animals and drag them away. Sometimes they attack baby elephants. They hunt alone and often travel 10 to 20km (6 to 12 miles) a night to find food. Only about one hunt in 20 is successful. If they cannot find big animals, they eat small ones, such as ants or frogs. They each eat about six tonnes (6½ tons) of meat a year, about the same amount of meat as in over 58,000 hamburgers.

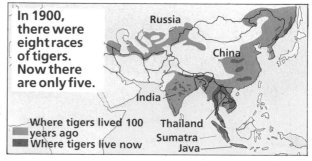

In 1900, there were eight races of tigers. Now there are only five.

Russia
China
India
Thailand
Sumatra
Java

■ Where tigers lived 100 years ago
■ Where tigers live now

When a tiger sees an animal, it hides a short distance away, waiting to attack.

It moves forward slowly, and when it gets near enough it rushes forward.

It pounces on the animal from the side or from the back and digs its claws in.

The animal falls down and the tiger bites it in the neck or throat to kill it.

Sometimes, when a tiger kills a large animal, other tigers come and eat it too.

Cat sizes

Here you can see how long some cats are when you compare them with each other.

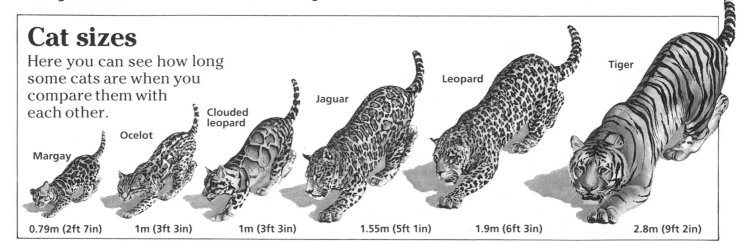

Margay
Ocelot
Clouded leopard
Jaguar
Leopard
Tiger

0.79m (2ft 7in) 1m (3ft 3in) 1m (3ft 3in) 1.55m (5ft 1in) 1.9m (6ft 3in) 2.8m (9ft 2in)

51

Rivers and streams

Rivers and streams run through every rainforest in the world. The River Amazon in South America is 6,400km (4,000 miles) long. It is mostly 2 to 5km (1 to 3 miles) wide, but near the sea, it can be as much as 320km (200 miles) wide. It is home to thousands of species of plants and animals, some of which you can see here. Deep in the forest, the main river splits up into over a thousand smaller rivers and streams.

In the rainy season the Amazon overflows and floods the nearby forest for up to 6 months.

Forest that becomes flooded

Unflooded forest

Level of river in rainy season

Normal level of river

Capybaras are the world's largest rodents. Like other rodents, such as guinea pigs and rats, they have large front teeth for gnawing.

Capybaras

Otter cubs

Dolphins

Giant otters live in groups of up to 15. They build dens in the river bank, and mark their home range with droppings. When swimming, they hum and chuckle to each other. They scream when scared.

Otters hold fish in their paws when they eat them.

Caimans, a type of crocodile, are now rare because people hunt them for their skins and steal their eggs.

Caimans

Under the water

There are 2,000 to 3,000 species of fish in the Amazon - ten times as many as in Europe. Some eat small animals and other fish. Others eat fruit and seeds that fall into the water.

Most piranhas eat seeds and nuts, but some eat meat. These swim in large groups and can eat an animal in a few minutes.

Piranhas

Tambaqui fish can eat up to 1kg (2.2lbs) of seeds each time they feed.

Teeth and jaws crush seeds

Tambaqui fish

Arapaima

Arapaimas are the biggest freshwater fish in the world. They grow to at least 3m (9 ft 10in) long and weigh up to 200kg (440lbs).

Blue and yellow macaws

Red uakari monkeys

Mangrove swamps

Forests change near the ocean. The river is salty and its level falls and rises with the ocean tides. The ground is always muddy. Tree roots cannot take in oxygen from mud, so they grow above the ground and take oxygen from the air. These areas near the ocean are called mangrove swamps. Here are some of the animals that live there.

Water at low tide

Mangrove tree roots

Fiddler crab

Male fiddler crabs have a big claw which they wave at females.

Mudskippers are fish which can live in and out of water. They twitch their bodies to jump around on tree roots.

Mudskipper

Anableps

Anableps have eyes which are split in two so they can see above and below the water at the same time.

There are 2 types of Amazon River dolphins. They are nearly blind and find their way by echo-location, like bats, sending out rapid clicks through the water. They may also "talk" to each other with clicks.

Red ibises

Red ibises are wading birds. They poke their beaks into the mud to search for food.

Manatees are the largest animals in the river. They grow up to 2.5m (8ft 2in) long. Scientists think they are distant relatives of elephants.

Nostrils

Amazon kingfisher

Electric eel

Manatee

Electric eels kill fish and other animals with shocks of up to 650 volts, enough to stun a horse.

Manatees eat about 20kg (44lbs) of plants a day. They close their nostrils under water and can stay there for an hour at a time. They taste and smell things with their tongues.

53

Reptiles and amphibians

Hundreds of different species of reptiles and amphibians live in rainforests. They live on the ground, in the trees, in and near water and even inside plants. Reptiles are scaly animals such as crocodiles, snakes and lizards which mainly live on land. Amphibians, such as frogs and toads, can live both in and out of water. You can see some of these animals here.

Snakes

Snakes live in trees and on the ground. Some use poison to kill their prey. The poison comes through their sharp teeth, called fangs. All snakes can open their mouths very wide to eat prey. If the prey is big their stomachs stretch so that it fits. Most snakes only need to eat about nine times a year.

Some snakes push the tube that they breathe through to the front of their mouths when they eat. This helps them breathe.

Breathing tube

Poison sac

Muscle stretches so jaw bones can separate.

Fangs

Upper jaw

Lower jaw

The fer de lance is the most poisonous snake in South America.

A snake's upper and lower jaw can come apart so they can stretch their mouths to swallow big prey.

Emerald tree boa

Emerald tree boas have prehensile tails. They use them to hang from branches and catch passing birds.

Anaconda

Gaboon viper

Snakes flick their tongues in and out to pick up smells in the air. They can recognize the smells of different animals and follow smells to find food or a mate.

An anaconda can open its mouth incredibly wide to eat big prey.

Caiman

Anacondas live near rivers. They are among the world's biggest snakes. They can grow up to 12m (39ft) long. Like some other big snakes, they kill by wrapping themselves tightly around their prey to stop it from breathing. They even kill and eat caimans.

Laying eggs

Most frogs and toads lay eggs in or near water and leave them. The eggs hatch into tadpoles which slowly change into tiny frogs or toads. In some cases, however, the adults look after their eggs and young.

Vocal sac

Male Darwin frogs keep their eggs in their vocal sacs. The eggs hatch and the frogs hop out when they have grown.

Hole

Male Surinam toads put their eggs in holes on the female's back where they hatch straight into toads.

Arrow-poison frogs carry their tadpoles from where they hatch.

They put each tadpole into a water-filled plant in the canopy.

The female feeds them each week with eggs that will not grow.

The tadpoles slowly grow into frogs in these tiny ponds.

Avoiding danger

Reptiles and amphibians have many ways of avoiding being eaten.

Arrow-poison frog

Arrow-poison frogs have different bright patterns to warn predators that they are very poisonous.

Some lizards, such as skinks, make their tails fall off if they are attacked. This confuses the predator and the lizard escapes.

Skink

Turtles have hard shells to protect them. Matamata turtles have bumpy shells which look like dead leaves.

Matamata turtle

Chameleon

Chameleons take on the colour of their surroundings so they cannot be seen easily.

Crocodiles

Crocodiles and alligators have hardly changed in 65 million years. They bask in the sun by rivers during the day. When it gets dark, they slide into the river to spend the night hunting in the water. They eat fish and insects, but also much bigger animals.

Nests are 2-3m (6-10ft) high.

See-through eyelids cover a crocodile's eyes under water. A flap of skin covers the back of its throat to stop it from swallowing water.

A crocodile uses its webbed feet for paddling slowly. It moves its strong tail from side to side when it swims fast.

A crocodile's eyes and nostrils are almost on top of its head so it can see and breathe when it is halfway under the water.

Some crocodiles make big nests to keep their eggs warm. Others bury their eggs in the ground. The young dig their way out when they hatch.

Insects and spiders

At least two-thirds of all living species on Earth are spiders and insects. Some of the most amazing and beautiful ones live in rainforests. Insects are always in danger of being eaten by larger animals, so many of them have ways of blending in with their surroundings which makes it more difficult for predators to spot them.

Some moths look like parts of trees.

This mantis looks like the flower it lives in.

This katydid looks like a leaf.

Beetles and butterflies

Most butterflies and beetles live in the tropics. There are so many that some do not have everyday names, only a scientific one. (These names are written in *italics*.) Butterflies live in the canopy, near flowers and water. Beetles live everywhere in the forest. Over 500 species of beetles can be found in one tree.

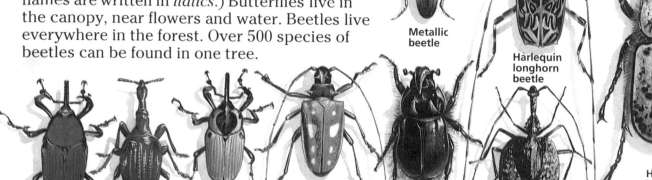

Metallic beetle

Harlequin longhorn beetle

Hercules beetle

Giant weevil Giraffe weevil Palm weevil Longhorn beetle Rhinoceros beetle Violin beetle

Agrias aedon

Papilio karna

Agrias claudina

Perisama vaninka

Idea jasonia

Callicore mengeli Callicore cyllene Callicore cajetani Perisama eminens

Agrias claudina Callithea optima Callithea davisi

Butterfly disguises

Many butterflies have very vivid patterns to warn predators that they taste unpleasant. Some harmless butterflies copy the appearance of bad tasting ones to trick predators into leaving them alone. Sometimes females of the same species do not look alike because in different places they copy the warning patterns of different types of poisonous butterflies.

Male mocker swallowtail butterfly from Africa

Female mocker swallowtail butterflies

Hunting spiders

Spiders are predators. Thousands of species live in rainforests. They hunt their food in different ways. Many of them catch insects and even small birds or reptiles in webs made out of spider silk. They kill their prey by biting it. Some spiders bite poison into their prey to stop it from struggling. Others wrap it up in silk. The silk comes from the spiders' bodies. It dries hard as soon as it reaches the air. Some spiders can make as much as 300m (nearly 1,000ft) of silk a day.

Wandering spider

Hairy body

Fangs

Tree frog

Spiders cannot eat solid food so they bite special juices into their prey to make its insides become liquid.

Large wandering spiders are about 8cm (3in) long. They hunt at night, catching insects and other small animals, such as tree frogs.

Crab spider

Nephila spiders make very strong silk which can even trap small animals. Some local fishermen use their silk to make fishing nets.

Gladiator spiders weave sticky silk nets which they drop onto their prey as it passes below them.

Argiope spiders spin patterned webs. Insects mistake the patterns for flowers and fly into the webs.

Crab spiders match the flowers they live in. They wait for insects to come to feed and then kill them.

Trapdoor tricks

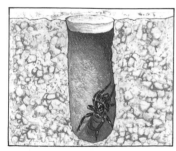

A trapdoor spider lives in a silk-lined burrow with a trapdoor entrance.

It lies in wait just under the door, sometimes with its legs sticking out.

It feels the ground move when an insect passes and rushes out to attack it.

It kills the insect and drags it in. It sucks out the insect's insides.

57

The rainforest floor

Animals that live on the rainforest floor are not often seen by people. Some only come out at night. Others are very small, or patterned so that they match their habitat and are difficult to see. Most of them feed on plants, roots, fallen fruit, insects or dead wood and leaves.

Forest elephants from India and Southeast Asia have small ears and short tusks. They use their trunks to reach for leaves on trees. Sometimes, if they cannot reach high enough, they push over small trees.

Asian elephant

Sumatran rhinoceros

Okapi

Okapis in Africa are related to giraffes. Their striped markings make them hard to see in the forest.

Agouti

Forest rhinos live in Southeast Asia. They eat leaves, can run fast and use their horns to fight.

Porcupine

Malaysian porcupines have sharp spines. When they attack, they raise their spines, rattle their spiny tails and charge backward at their enemy.

Peccary

Peccaries and agoutis sniff around on the ground looking for plant roots, nuts and seeds. They are the only animals, apart from parrots, that can crack open the hard shells of Brazil nuts.

Pangolin

Royal antelope

Goliath frog

Royal antelopes in Africa are 30cm (1ft) tall and weigh 2.5kg (5.5lbs). This is less than African Goliath frogs which weigh up to 3.1kg (6.8lbs).

Pangolins are covered in hard scales which predators cannot bite through. They use their long tongues to lick up ants and termites. Some species live mainly on the ground. Others live in trees.

Birds on the ground

Many birds spend a great deal of time on the ground. They may fly up into the trees to escape from predators.

Peacocks live in Southeast Asia. The males display their beautiful feathers to show off to females.

These are jungle fowl. Domestic chickens are descended from them.

Great argus pheasants have tail feathers which are 1 to 1.5m (3 to 5ft) long.

Megapode birds

Megapode birds have big feet, which they use to push soil and leaves together to make big mounds. They bury their eggs inside these mounds.

The mounds are about 1.5m (5ft) high. The eggs are kept warm by the sun and by heat from the dead leaves which start to rot in the soil.

The male bird tests the temperature of the mound with his beak. If it is too hot or too cold, he takes away or adds some soil.

The chicks dig their way out and run off after they hatch. They fly within a few hours. The parents do not look after them at all.

Ants and termites

Many insects, such as ants and termites, live on the forest floor in large groups called colonies. Some termites live in rotting wood and others build mounds out of soil, their own droppings and saliva.

The queen is huge. She mates with the king. She is the only one that can lay eggs. She lays thousands of eggs every day.

Queen

King

Workers

Soldier

Soldier termites defend the colony. They have bigger heads and jaws than workers.

Termites called workers build the mound, find food and look after the queen.

Some workers grow food for the colony. They build their droppings into structures called combs. Fungus grows on the combs. Then the termites eat both the fungus and the combs.

Inside a termite mound

Strong, hard walls made out of droppings, saliva and soil

Fungus chamber

Comb

Royal chamber for king and queen

Rainforest people

People have been living in groups, called tribes, in rainforests for about 40,000 years. The forest provides them with everything they need to survive. They hunt animals, gather plants and fruit, and some tribes grow crops. They build their homes out of parts of trees and plants and know how to use hundreds of different plants as medicines.

The Penan tribe live in Sarawak in Malaysia.

The Kayapo Indians are a tribe that live in Brazil.

Yanomami Indians

Area where the Yanomami live

The Yanomami Indians live in Brazil in small villages. In each village all the people live in one big, round house called a yano. Yanos are always built close to rivers and are surrounded by gardens where the villagers grow up to 60 different crops. Half the gardens are planted with banana and plantain trees. The rest are planted with other crops, such as corn, cassava (a root vegetable), sweet potatoes, and fruit, such as papaya. Only about 20 crops are used for food, the rest are used for medicines, religious ceremonies, or for making things.

Women look after the crops and gather food from the forest.

Each family has a fire which they keep burning day and night.

Yano

The Yanomami keep pets such as monkeys and macaws.

The central space is used for dancing and ceremonies.

A yano is made from trees. The roof is made of palm leaves.

Families live under the roofed part of the yano. They sleep in hammocks.

Bananas and plantains are often eaten. They are roasted, boiled or made into soup.

Women dry, grate and sieve cassava (also called manioc) to make a kind of bread.

Hunting

Yanomami men go hunting almost every day. Boys start to go hunting when they are about five years old. Each morning the hunters go into the forest alone or in groups of two or three. They hunt with large blowpipes, bows and poison-tipped arrows. It takes a long time for a hunter to learn how to use weapons well. Good hunters are highly respected in the tribe.

The Yanomamis hunt with very big weapons.

Shamans

The Yanomami Indians believe that everything has a spirit and that these spirits can affect their everyday lives. Spirits must be respected otherwise they will cause illness and other troubles which can only be cured by healers, called shamans. When someone is ill, a shaman dances and sings to call good spirits down from the sky to help find out which bad spirit is causing the illness. The good spirits help send the bad spirits away so the ill person gets well.

Before a healing ceremony, a shaman paints his body and breathes in a special powder which makes him see visions.

A shaman dances and chants to a bad spirit calling it out of an ill person's body. This ceremony can last many hours.

A shaman dancing

Feasts and stories

Members of a village often invite friends and family from other places to a feast. It takes several days to get the feast ready. Before the feast, the Yanomami paint patterns on their bodies. The feast may last many days. It is a Yanomami custom to be very generous. Both villages give each other presents and there is a lot of singing, dancing and story telling. Here is a story about how some birds got red feathers.

One day two girls came to the home of Opossum and his mother, the Mushroom Woman. He offered them food but they said it all smelled bad.

He sent them to a friend's home to get some tobacco. The friend, a man called Honey, was so handsome that the girls forgot about Opossum.

Opossum became jealous and that night he shot Honey with a magic dart and killed him. Soon everyone knew about this.

Opossum was so scared he grew feathers and flew away, but the birds, led by Toucan, found and killed him and painted themselves with his blood.

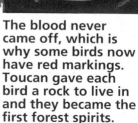

The blood never came off, which is why some birds now have red markings. Toucan gave each bird a rock to live in and they became the first forest spirits.

61

Rainforests in danger

Rainforest people, animals and plants are dying out because the forests are being cut down to make room to grow crops, to farm cattle, to search for coal and precious metals in the ground, or to sell the wood from the trees. If this continues, rainforests will disappear forever and many things, such as the weather, will change. Many people, plants and animals have already died out and many others are in danger.

The animals shown here are all endangered species. This means that there are very few of them left in the wild and they could easily die out.

Hyacinth macaw

A third of all parrots are endangered, including hyacinth macaws, the largest parrots in the world.

Golden lion tamarin

Golden lion tamarins are among the most endangered species of monkeys in the world.

Homerus swallowtail butterfly

Humboldt's woolly monkeys have been hunted almost to extinction.

Humboldt's woolly monkey

Homerus swallowtail butterflies are among the world's rarest butterflies.

Plants and medicines

Rainforests provide many things which we use. For example, many of our foods come from rainforests. Over a quarter of all medicines are made out of rainforest plants and there are still thousands of plants that scientists and doctors do not know about. It would be better to learn how to use things from the rainforests without damaging them, than to cut them all down so that there are none left in the future.

62

Bananas

Rice

Coffee

Oranges

Pineapple

Avocados

Lemons

Many foods come from plants that first grew in rainforests.

A medicine made out of rosy periwinkles from Madagascar is used to treat a type of cancer called leukaemia.

Rosy periwinkle

Saving the rainforest

There are some things being done to save rainforests. Areas of land called national parks, or reserves, have been set aside where people, animals, and plants can live safely. Projects are being set up to save some species of animals and plants which are very rare. Some laws have been passed to protect rainforests and rare animals.

Mountain gorillas live in national parks on the borders of Rwanda, Zaire and Uganda in Africa. By 1978 they were almost extinct, and some conservation groups and the government of Rwanda, set up the Mountain Gorilla Project to try to save them. They organized guards to protect the gorillas from hunters, taught local people how important the gorillas were and set up tourist trips to help make money for the park. The gorillas and their habitat are now safe.

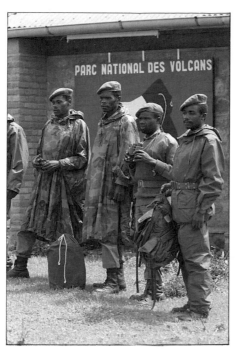

Local people work in the Rwandan national park. It is now important to Rwanda because it makes money.

Since 1960, miners and road builders have been working in the Brazilian rainforest. They have cut down a lot of forest and many Yanomami Indians have lost their homes. Some have also caught diseases, such as mumps, from the workers, and died. Survival International (see right) set up a campaign to try to save the Yanomami. In 1991, the president of Brazil finally agreed to turn Yanomami lands into a national park.

In 1983, people from 13 Yanomami villages died from disease when a road was built through their lands.

Joining a group

There are many international groups who work to save the rainforests and the people and animals that live there. You can become a member and find out what you can do to help.

Survival International is a worldwide organization which helps tribal people. It believes they should decide their own future and helps them to save their homes and way of life.

For more information write to:

**Survival International,
310 Edgware Road,
London W2 1DY,
UK**

This is the symbol of Survival International.

The World Wide Fund for Nature (WWF)* teaches people about looking after nature and raises money to protect species and habitats all around the world.

For more information write to:

**Information Division,
WWF International,
Avenue du Mont-Blanc,
CH-1196 Gland,
Switzerland**

The giant panda is the symbol of the WWF.

The International Council for Bird Preservation (ICBP) works to save endangered birds.

For more information write to:

**ICBP,
32 Cambridge Road,
Girton,
Cambridge,
CB3 0PJ,
UK**

This is the symbol of the ICBP.

*USA and Canada = World Wildlife Fund   63

GRASSLAND WILDLIFE

Kamini Khanduri

Scientific consultant: David Duthie

Contents

Grassland areas

Grasslands are large, open areas of land, covered in grass. Low bushes and a few trees may also grow there. Today, many grassland areas are used by people as farmland, but in places where people do not farm, grasslands are home to lots of different kinds of wild plants and animals. The big picture below shows a hot African grassland, and some of the exciting wildlife that lives there.

Fires in grasslands are often started by sparks of lightning during storms. When it has not rained for a long time, the grass, bushes and trees are very dry, so they catch fire easily and burn quickly.

Trees and grasses

Trees need a lot of water. There is not much rain in grassland areas so most species (kinds) of trees cannot grow there. The few trees which do grow have special ways of surviving at dry times of the year.

Baobab tree with swollen trunk

Whenever it rains, baobab trees take up lots of water from the soil. They store the water inside their trunks which look very swollen.

Grasses do not need as much water as taller plants, so about 10,000 different species grow in grasslands. These three species grow in North America.

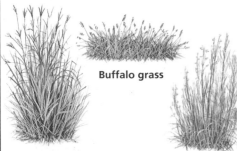

Buffalo grass

Big bluestem grass

Little bluestem grass

Acacia tree

Trees provide food and shelter for animals.

Giraffes

Cattle egrets

Buffaloes

Elephants

When it has not rained for a long time, animals gather at areas of water, called waterholes. These may be very far apart.

Antelopes

Zebras

Many plant-eating animals, such as zebras and antelopes, live in groups. They are safer from enemies if they stay together.

Puff adder

Reptiles, such as snakes and lizards, live among the grasses, or on rocks.

Grasslands of the world

Grasslands cover about a quarter of the world. This map shows where they are. There are two kinds of grassland areas - tropical and temperate. In tropical areas, it is hot all year long with two seasons - a rainy one and a dry one. In temperate areas, there are four seasons, with hot summers and cold winters.

NORTH AMERICA

EUROPE

ASIA

AFRICA

SOUTH AMERICA

AUSTRALIA

European and Asian temperate grasslands are called steppes.

North American grasslands are called prairies.

Tropic of Cancer

Equator

Grasslands between these two lines are tropical grasslands, or savannas. Grasslands outside this area are temperate grasslands.

Tropic of Capricorn

South American temperate grasslands are called pampas.

Much of the wildlife in African grasslands is protected in huge parks.

Grassland areas

Ostriches

Insects called termites build nests inside huge mounds of soil. Thousands of them live inside.

Termite mound

Baboons live in groups, called troops. They eat mainly plants but they hunt too.

Baboons

Female lion with cubs

Meat-eaters, such as lions, hunt other animals. Lions are the only cats that live in groups.

Rocky areas, called kopjes (pronounced "koppees"), provide good hiding places for animals.

Agama lizard

Plant-eaters

All kinds of animals feed on the grasses, bushes and trees that grow in grasslands. Plant-eating animals are called herbivores. They have to eat more often than meat-eaters because plants do not contain as much nourishment as meat. Many herbivores spend almost all day feeding, or looking for food.

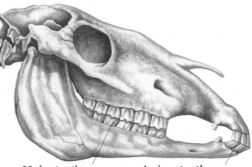

Molar teeth are used for grinding and chewing.

Incisor teeth are used for cutting and gnawing.

This picture shows a zebra's skull. Like most herbivores, zebras have strong teeth to cut and grind tough plants.

Kangaroos

Kangaroos live in Australian grasslands, in groups called mobs. There are 14 different species. Instead of running, kangaroos jump along on their back legs, using their tails to help them balance. When they are feeding, they lean forward onto all fours and move slowly along. They usually feed during the night and grasses are their main food. Kangaroos are marsupials (animals that carry their babies in pouches). Baby kangaroos are called joeys.

This female grey kangaroo is carrying her baby in her pouch. The baby feeds on milk from a nipple inside the pouch.

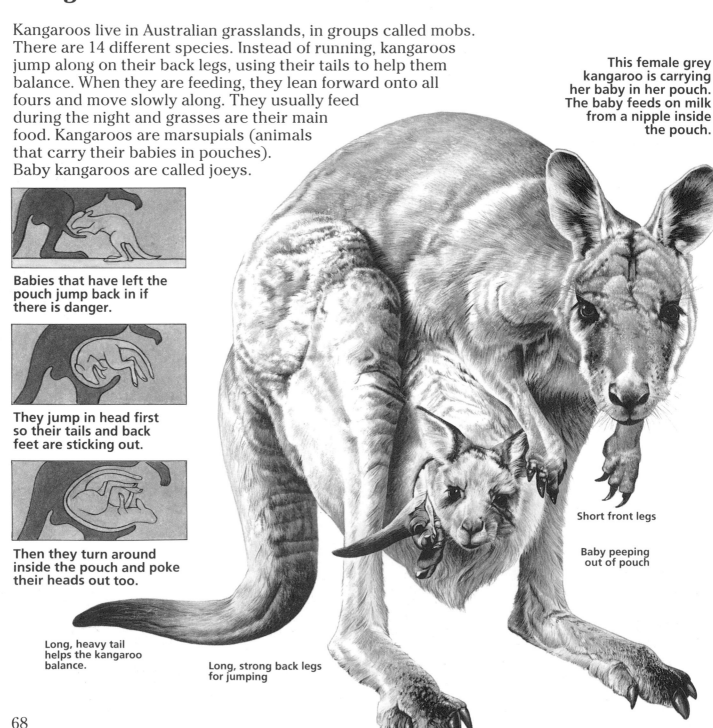

Babies that have left the pouch jump back in if there is danger.

They jump in head first so their tails and back feet are sticking out.

Then they turn around inside the pouch and poke their heads out too.

Long, heavy tail helps the kangaroo balance.

Long, strong back legs for jumping

Short front legs

Baby peeping out of pouch

Food for all

Different herbivores feed on different plants, or on different parts of the same plant. This means that more species can live in one area without competing for food. Animals that feed on grasses are called grazers. Animals that feed on bushes or trees are called browsers. Some animals are both grazers and browsers. The animals in this picture live in African savannas. (They would not really be found so close together.)

Elephants stretch their trunks up to browse on leaves, twigs and branches. They also reach down to the ground to pull up grasses.

Gerenuks, a species of antelope, can stand up on their back legs to browse on leaves from bushes.

Warthogs pluck short grasses with their teeth and lips.

Giraffes have long necks so they can browse on the top parts of trees. They pull off leaves and twigs with their lips and tongues.

Male giraffes stretch up to reach leaves above their heads.

Female giraffes browse on leaves just below their mouths.

Black rhinos browse on leaves from bushes at the same level as their heads.

Dik-diks, the smallest antelopes, browse on the lowest parts of bushes.

Rodents

Rodents have long, sharp incisor teeth so they can gnaw through very tough plants. Many species of rodents live in grasslands. They often live in large groups. (These pictures are not to scale.)

Maras live in South American pampas.

Gophers live in North American prairies.

Naked mole-rats live in burrows in African savannas.

Susliks live in Asian steppes.

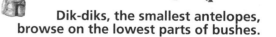

Antelopes

Antelopes are related to deer. About 50 species live in grasslands, or feed there during part of the year. Some are grazers and some are browsers. Most can run very fast to escape from enemies. All the antelopes shown here live in African savannas, except for the pronghorn which lives in North American prairies, and the saiga which lives in Asian steppes.

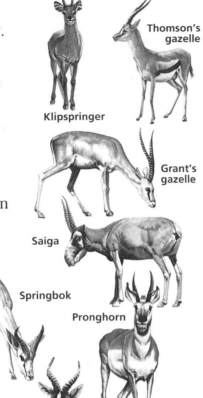

Klipspringer

Thomson's gazelle

Grant's gazelle

Saiga

Impala

Springbok

Pronghorn

Kob

Bontebok

Blesbok

Topi

Waterbuck

Wildebeest

Hartebeest

Common eland

Roan antelope

Problems for plants

The leaves of grassland plants are always being eaten by animals. Grasses are better at surviving this than trees. They have long, straight leaves that grow upward from the bottom of the plant. The tops of the leaves are eaten, but the growing parts near the ground are left untouched.

When an animal bites off grass leaves from the top, the leaves keep growing from the bottom. In time, the same leaves grow tall again.

When an animal feeds on a tree's leaves, it eats the whole leaf, including the growing part, so the tree has to grow new leaves. Some trees have ways of protecting their leaves from animals.

Acacia trees have long, spiky thorns on their branches. This stops some animals from eating their leaves. Some species of acacias also have nasty-tasting leaves.

Elephants sometimes destroy whole trees while they are feeding.

Elephants

Elephants are the largest land animals. They can live for up to 60 years and have an amazing ability to learn and remember things. On African savannas, elephants live in family groups. They travel long distances each day, in search of food, water and shady trees. They need to eat a lot, because they are so big. All the elephants in this part of the book are African elephants.

Female African elephant

An elephant's tusks are long incisor teeth. They first appear at around the age of two and go on growing all through the elephant's life. Elephants use their tusks to scrape bark off trees and to dig for roots.

Baby African elephant

Hyraxes are related to elephants, although they look nothing like them. They are about the size of big rabbits and they live on kopjes.

Baby elephants are called calves. They are usually very playful. They feed on their mother's milk until they are three or four years old.

Useful noses

An elephant's trunk is its nose. There are two nostrils at the end of it. Trunks are very useful.

Two "lips" at the end of the trunk are used like fingers to pick things up and to pluck grass.

Elephants suck water into their trunks and squirt it into their mouths or over their bodies.

When they meet, elephants often touch each other with their trunks, as a greeting.

Mothers often stroke their babies with their trunks, and gently guide them along.

Meat-eaters

Animals that eat meat are called carnivores. Carnivores that hunt other animals are called predators and the animals they hunt are called prey. Most predators have sharp eyesight and hearing, and a good sense of smell. Wherever they live, carnivores depend on other animals for food. The animals they eat may be carnivores themselves, or herbivores. One way of showing who eats what in a particular area is by a food web. The picture below shows part of a food web in a North American prairie. (The pictures are not to scale.)

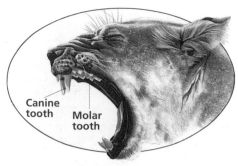

Canine tooth   Molar tooth

Lions have teeth that are well-suited to eating meat. They kill prey with their long canine teeth and slice it up with their sharp molar teeth.

An arrow from one thing to another means the first is eaten by the second. For example, mice are eaten by skunks, and skunks are eaten by golden eagles.

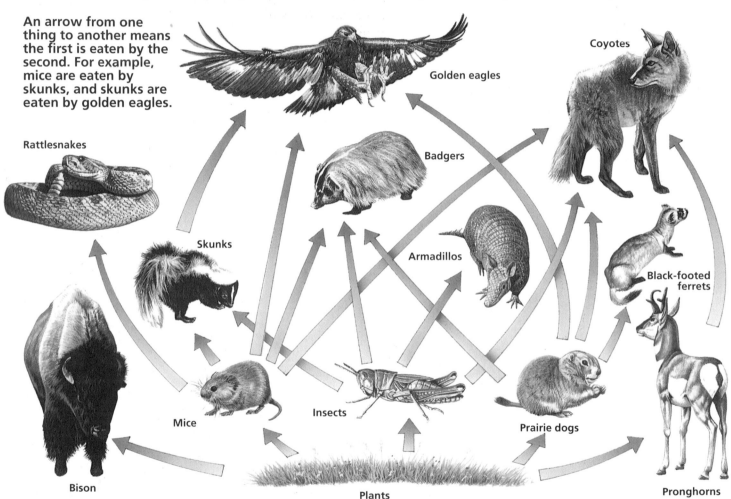

Rattlesnakes

Golden eagles

Coyotes

Badgers

Skunks

Armadillos

Black-footed ferrets

Mice

Insects

Prairie dogs

Bison

Plants

Pronghorns

Hunting in burrows

In temperate grasslands, many small animals live underground. They run into their burrows when they see a predator approaching. During the winter, they may not come out at all. Some predators can find these animals even inside their burrows. They have to use their sense of smell because it is too dark to see clearly.

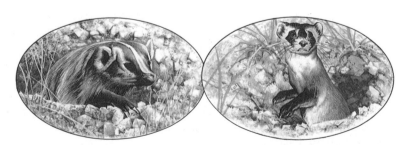

American badgers dig out small animals, such as mice and prairie dogs, from their burrows.

Black-footed ferrets chase prairie dogs into their burrows and hunt them underground.

Wild dogs

African wild dogs live in groups, called packs, of up to 30 members. They travel over huge areas in search of food. They hunt in the cool early morning or in the evening shade, feeding mainly on Thomson's gazelles, wildebeest and zebras. The whole pack hunts together, working as a team. This means they can catch larger prey than a single dog could. These pictures show a pack of dogs hunting wildebeest.

The dogs spot the wildebeest from a distance and approach slowly at first.

The wildebeest scatter in all directions as soon as they see the dogs. Most of them manage to escape.

The dogs start to run. They can run fast - up to 70kph (44mph).

Early in the hunt, the dogs pick one of the wildebeest to chase - usually a young, old or sick animal.

When the dogs catch the wildebeest, they attack it from underneath.

After killing the wildebeest, all the dogs share the meal. The older dogs usually let the younger ones feed first.

73

Cheetahs

Cheetahs live in African savannas. The females live alone except when they have babies. The males often live in small groups of two or three. Cheetahs can run at speeds of up to 110kph (68mph) and are the world's fastest land animals. They hunt alone during the day, feeding mainly on Thomson's gazelles. Although they can run fast, they cannot keep up this speed for long, so they stalk their prey for up to three hours before starting to chase it. Only about half their chases are successful.

Cheetahs often climb up onto termite mounds to get a better view of the area around them. They have excellent eyesight.

This cheetah is stalking a gazelle. If the gazelle looks up, the cheetah stops and stands absolutely still. The gazelle cannot easily see it among the tall grasses.

When it is about 30m (100ft) from the gazelle, the cheetah springs forward into a run. The gazelle runs too. The chase hardly ever lasts longer than a minute.

If it catches up with the gazelle, the cheetah trips it over with its paw and kills it by biting its throat. Then it drags it away to a hiding place before eating it.

Small, rounded head

Small, flattish ears

Cheetah cubs

Cheetahs usually have three babies at a time. Baby cheetahs, called cubs, are very playful. They climb around and even jump onto their mother's back. Cubs stay with their mother for about 18 months.

Female cheetah

Cheetahs are slim, graceful cats with strong muscles and long legs. They have small, round, black spots on their coats and black stripes running down the sides of their noses.

Storing food

Predators often cannot eat the whole of a kill at once. Some species hide the remains of their food, or store it where other animals cannot get to it. They return to these hiding places when they are hungry again.

Hyenas often hide their leftover food in holes in the ground or muddy pools.

Leopards drag their prey up into trees. They eat what they can and store the remains among the branches.

Scavengers

Carnivores do not always kill their own food. Sometimes they feed on animals that have been killed by other animals, or have died naturally. This is called scavenging. It means that nothing is wasted and the ground is kept clear of carcasses (the bodies of dead animals). Many predators, such as lions and wild dogs, often scavenge too. The picture below shows hyenas, jackals and vultures scavenging on a zebra carcass. Vultures get nearly all their food by scavenging. Different species feed in different ways.

Lappet-faced vultures are very strong, with big, sharp beaks. They can rip up tough skin and muscle that other species cannot feed on.

White-backed vultures stick their heads right inside a carcass to feed. The feathers on their heads are short so they do not get too dirty.

Egyptian vultures stand away from the carcass, waiting to feed on scraps of food that have been torn off and tossed aside by larger species.

Egyptian vultures

Hyenas have strong jaws to crack open bones and feed on the marrow inside.

Spotted hyena

Lappet-faced vulture

Vultures are often the first to spot a dead animal. They see it from the sky and fly down immediately.

Hyenas and jackals get some of their food by scavenging but they often hunt too.

Zebra carcass

White-backed vulture

Golden jackal

A group of scavengers may take only a few minutes to finish a carcass, leaving nothing but a pile of bones.

The changing seasons

During the dry season in tropical grasslands, areas of water dry up, trees lose their leaves and grasses stop growing. Some animals have to travel long distances to find food and water. These journeys are called migrations. The most spectacular migrations are those of wildebeest and zebras in the Serengeti National Park in Tanzania, Africa.

Wildebeest

Zebras

Migration routes

The map below shows the migration routes of animals in the Serengeti National Park. Thomson's gazelles migrate with wildebeest and zebras. These three species eat different parts of the same grasses, so they can feed in the same area without competing for food.

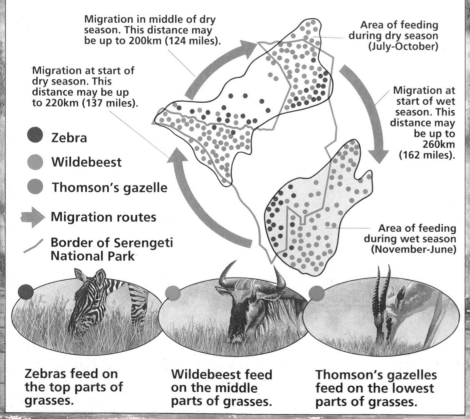

Migration in middle of dry season. This distance may be up to 200km (124 miles).

Area of feeding during dry season (July-October)

Migration at start of dry season. This distance may be up to 220km (137 miles).

Migration at start of wet season. This distance may be up to 260km (162 miles).

● Zebra

● Wildebeest

● Thomson's gazelle

➤ Migration routes

╱ Border of Serengeti National Park

Area of feeding during wet season (November-June)

Zebras feed on the top parts of grasses.

Wildebeest feed on the middle parts of grasses.

Thomson's gazelles feed on the lowest parts of grasses.

Up to a million wildebeest and thousands of zebras migrate together. Their trampling hoofs make paths in the soil.

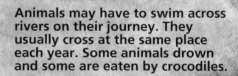

Animals may have to swim across rivers on their journey. They usually cross at the same place each year. Some animals drown and some are eaten by crocodiles.

Nile crocodile

Rainy days

At the start of the rainy season, dark clouds fill the sky. There is often lightning too.

Rain begins to fall, making pools of water on the dry ground. It rains for about two months.

Pools of water join together into lakes or marshy areas. Animals come to drink or play there.

After the rain, the grasses start to grow again and the trees grow new leaves.

In some years, called drought years, there is no rain. Thousands of animals may die of thirst or hunger.

Spotted hyenas

White-backed vultures

Predators, such as hyenas, often follow migrating herds for part of their journey. They usually catch old, young or weak animals.

Migrating animals may travel as far as 1,609km (1,000 miles) a year, and up to 80km (50 miles) in one day.

Hard winters

In temperate grasslands, the winters can be bitterly cold. Small animals burrow underground and stay there until spring. Larger animals have to survive in the open air. The ground is often covered with up to 50cm (20in) of snow and the temperature may be well below freezing point.

Bison have thick, shaggy coats to keep them warm. They dig under the snow, searching for plants.

77

Avoiding enemies

There are not many hiding places on grasslands, so animals have to find other ways of avoiding their enemies. Small animals, such as rodents, usually try to run into their burrows if there is danger. Very large animals, such as elephants and rhinos, are safe from most predators because of their size. Other animals have different ways of avoiding enemies.

Keeping a look-out

Animals have to look out for enemies all the time, to avoid being taken by surprise. This is easier for animals that live in groups. Together, they have more eyes, ears and noses to sense danger. In some species, such as dwarf mongooses, group members take turns as look-outs. If there is danger, the look-out gives loud warning calls and the rest of the group runs to hide.

Most herbivores have eyes on the sides of their heads, so they can see all around even while they are feeding with their heads down.

Dwarf mongoose

Dwarf mongooses often stand on termite mounds to look out for enemies. They have a better view from higher up.

Running away

Running away is the most common way of escaping from enemies.

Kangaroos jump along at speeds of up to 50kph (30mph).

Ostriches run along at speeds of up to 80kph (50mph).

Gazelles gallop along at speeds of up to 100kph (60mph).

Warning signals

Some animals give warning signals if they are in danger. This can let other members of their group know about the danger. It can also confuse an enemy so that it does not attack.

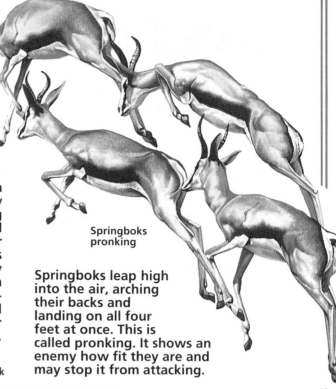

Springboks pronking

As they run, pronghorns fluff up the white hairs on their rumps. This flashes a warning to the rest of the herd.

Skunks warn enemies away by stamping their feet and raising their tails. If this does not work, they squirt them with a nasty-smelling liquid from under their tails.

Striped skunk

Springboks leap high into the air, arching their backs and landing on all four feet at once. This is called pronking. It shows an enemy how fit they are and may stop it from attacking.

Camouflage

Many animals match their surroundings. This is called camouflage. A lot of grassland animals are brown with stripes or patches, so they blend with grasses and bushes. If a camouflaged animal keeps still, predators cannot easily spot it.

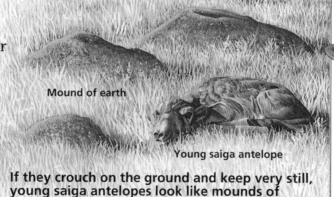

Mound of earth

Young saiga antelope

If they crouch on the ground and keep very still, young saiga antelopes look like mounds of earth. They do this when there is danger.

Fighting back

Instead of hiding or running away, some animals fight back, or turn to face their enemies.

Buffaloes facing an enemy

Buffaloes stand in a line, with their fierce-looking horns facing the enemy. The babies are protected between the adults.

Adult giraffes are safe from most predators because of their size, but babies are sometimes attacked. Mother giraffes protect their babies by kicking out at predators.

Giraffe kicking lion

Insects

These pages show some of the more unusual insects living in grasslands. Many common insects, such as ants, bees, wasps, butterflies and grasshoppers, live there too. Some insects eat plants and some bite other animals to feed on their blood. Many insects stay hidden in the soil, or among the grasses. Although they are small, insects are very important. The tiny tsetse fly in Africa is the main reason why people do not live or farm in some savanna areas.

When tsetse flies bite people or farm animals, they can give them diseases. Wild animals do not get these diseases.

Beetle balls

Dung beetles gather the dung (droppings) of other animals. Some species make the dung into balls. If a male and female beetle meet at a pile of dung, the male makes a ball. Then the two of them roll the ball as far as 15m (50ft). They eat some of the dung and bury the rest in their underground burrow. Then the female lays her eggs in it.

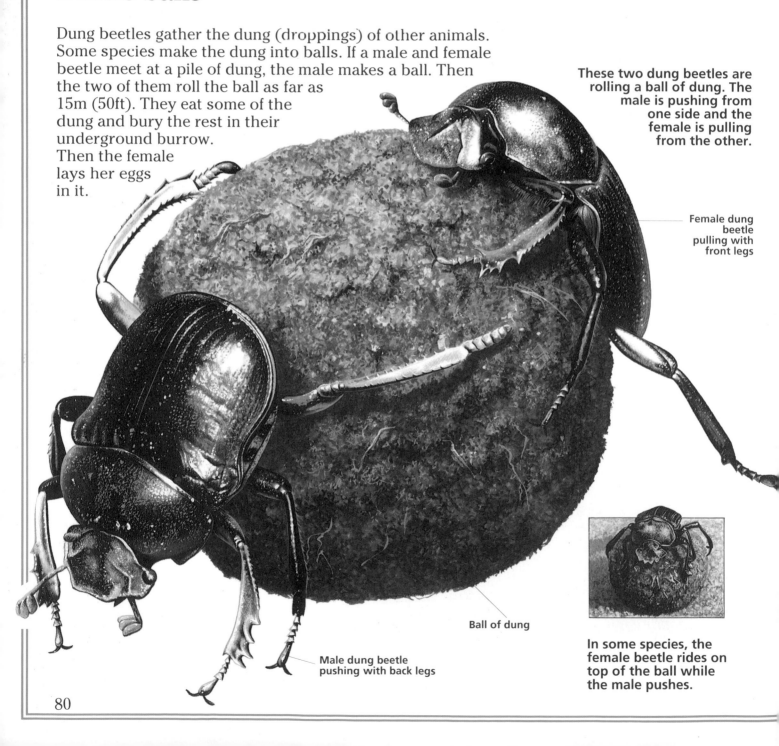

These two dung beetles are rolling a ball of dung. The male is pushing from one side and the female is pulling from the other.

Female dung beetle pulling with front legs

Ball of dung

Male dung beetle pushing with back legs

In some species, the female beetle rides on top of the ball while the male pushes.

Termite homes

Termites live mainly in tropical grasslands. Many species build nests inside huge mounds which they make out of soil, saliva and droppings. In each nest, there is one queen termite, one king termite and lots of soldiers and workers. Each type has a different job.

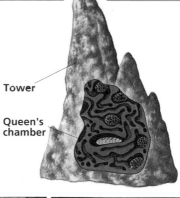

Tower

Queen's chamber

Inside the nest, there are lots of chambers (rooms), joined by tunnels. Tall, hollow towers up to 7.6m (25ft) high let fresh air in and stale air out.

Queen

The king and queen are the parents of all the other termites. The queen's body is so big, she cannot move at all.

The queen lays eggs all the time - up to 36,000 a day. The workers carry the eggs away to the nursery chambers.

The eggs hatch into tiny white larvae (young). The workers look after them. The larvae grow up to be workers or soldiers.

To feed the termites, the workers grow fungus in garden chambers. They also gather grass from outside the nest.

The soldiers have sharp jaws and huge heads, like helmets. They protect the nest from enemies, such as ants.

Swarming locusts

Locusts are a kind of grasshopper. They have strong jaws to chew tough leaves. When it rains, huge numbers swarm together to feed. There may be 1,000 million locusts in a swarm and each may eat its own weight in food every day. In farming areas, locusts do a lot of damage to crops.

Female locusts stretch the egg-laying part of their bodies to about twice its normal length, to lay their eggs deep in the soil.

Stretched part of locust's body

Eggs inside foamy liquid

Insect-eaters

These animals eat almost nothing but insects. They eat mainly ants and termites and can destroy whole nests.

Giant anteater

Aardvark

Aardvarks live in Africa. To feed, they push their long snouts into termite nests. They feed alone at night.

Giant anteaters live mainly in South America. They lick up termites with their long, sticky tongues.

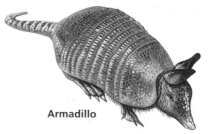

Armadillo

Armadillos live in North and South America. Their bodies are covered in hard, bony plates. These protect them from enemies.

Bat-eared foxes live in Africa. Their huge ears help them hear termites moving underground.

Bat-eared fox

Birds

Many different kinds of birds live in grasslands. Most birds feed on seeds or insects, so there is usually plenty of food for them there. Birds of prey, such as eagles and falcons, feed on other birds or on small animals, such as mice and other rodents. These pictures show some of the birds found in grasslands around the world.

Little bustard

Ground hornbill

Prairie falcon

Prairie chicken

Budgerigar

Yellow-bellied sunbird

Crested tinamou

Golden eagle

Meadow pipit

Saddlebill stork

Sulphur-crested cockatoo

Secretary bird

Horned lark

Pink-breasted galah

Emu

Black-necked screamer

Crowned crane

Bateleur eagle

Rhea

Lilac-breasted roller

Superb starling

Unusual feeders

Some birds feed on unusual types of food, or have unusual ways of getting their food.

Rufous-backed shrike

Some species of shrikes spike their prey onto thorns after they have killed it. This holds the prey firm while the shrike feeds on it.

Egyptian vultures

Locust stuck onto acacia thorn by shrike

Egyptian vultures break ostrich eggs by dropping stones onto them. Then they feed on the insides.

Helping each other

Small birds are often found on or near larger animals. Sometimes the bird is useful to the larger animal, sometimes the larger animal is useful to the bird and sometimes the two help each other.

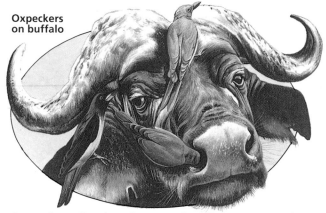

Oxpeckers on buffalo

Oxpeckers feed on insects that live on or under the skin of larger animals. These animals would not be able to remove the insects themselves.

Cattle egrets feed on insects that have been disturbed by the feet of larger animals. If they sense danger, the birds fly into the air, calling and warning the larger animal.

Cattle egrets with elephant

African honey guides are birds which feed on wax from bees' nests. They cannot open the nests themselves so they guide people, or other animals that eat honey, to the nest. These pictures show a honey guide leading a honey badger to a bees' nest.

The honey guide calls loudly and flutters around from tree to tree to attract the attention of the honey badger.

The badger follows the bird along. When the bird stops and falls silent, the badger looks for a bees' nest.

When the badger finds the nest, it tears it open and eats the honey. Then the bird flies down and eats the wax.

Courtship

When they are looking for a mate, male birds often dance or show off to attract females. This is called a courtship display. North American sage grouse do an amazing display. In the spring, lots of males gather on the prairie. For about two hours each day, in the early morning, they strut around, pretending to fight each other. This goes on for several weeks. The male that is best at strutting and fighting attracts the most females.

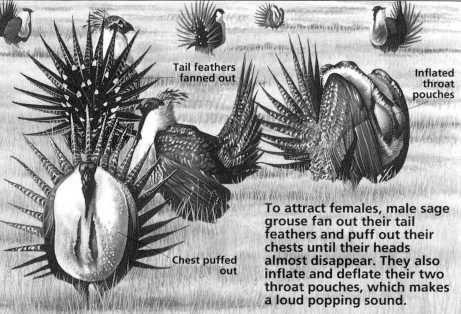

Tail feathers fanned out

Inflated throat pouches

Chest puffed out

To attract females, male sage grouse fan out their tail feathers and puff out their chests until their heads almost disappear. They also inflate and deflate their two throat pouches, which makes a loud popping sound.

Ostriches

Ostriches live in African savannas. They are the biggest birds in the world and can be up to 2.5m (8ft) tall - taller than a horse. Ostriches cannot fly, but they can run very fast to escape from predators. They feed mainly on grass and other plants. Both the males and the females look after the chicks.

Ostriches are so tall, they can see over the tops of bushes and long grass. This helps them to spot predators. They also have excellent eyesight.

Male ostrich

Long neck

Female ostrich

Ostrich chicks are speckled and striped. This helps them to stay hidden among the grass.

Ostrich chicks

Long, powerful legs help ostriches to run fast.

Ostriches only have two toes on each foot. Most birds have four.

To attract females, a male ostrich leans his head back and moves it quickly from side to side. He beats his wings and flutters his tail.

The male may mate with several females which all lay their eggs in one nest on the ground. Ostrich eggs are about 15cm (6 inches) long.

The male and one of the females take turns keeping the eggs warm. Eggs at the edge of the nest that are left uncovered get cold and do not hatch.

After about a month, chicks hatch out of the eggs. They can run almost immediately and both parents protect them from predators.

Safe nests

Because there are so few trees in grasslands, it is difficult for birds to find nesting places. Lots of birds of the same species may make their nests in one tree. Some birds make their nests on the ground. They have to guard their eggs and chicks carefully, so predators do not steal them. Some birds have ways of making safe nests.

Rufous ovenbird on nest

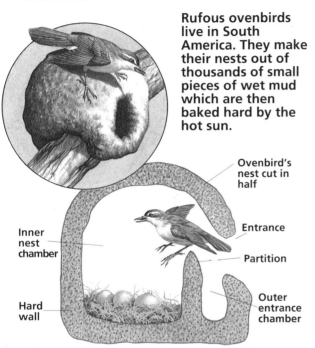

Rufous ovenbirds live in South America. They make their nests out of thousands of small pieces of wet mud which are then baked hard by the hot sun.

Ovenbird's nest cut in half

Inner nest chamber

Entrance

Partition

Hard wall

Outer entrance chamber

Inside an ovenbird's nest, there are two chambers with a partition between them. The ovenbirds can just fit over the top of the partition but larger predators cannot get into the nest chamber.

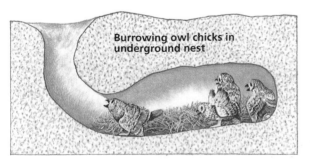

Burrowing owl chicks in underground nest

Burrowing owls live in North and South America. They make their nests in underground burrows. If a predator, such as a coyote, approaches, the owls make hissing noises. The coyote thinks there are snakes in the burrow and does not attack.

Amazing weavers

Weaverbirds make very complicated nests out of lots of pieces of grass. Different species make different shapes but the nests usually hang from a branch. It is the male that makes the nest.

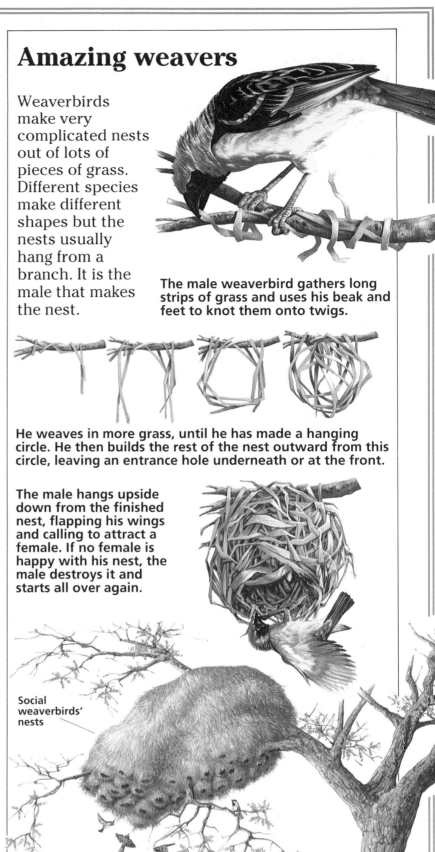

The male weaverbird gathers long strips of grass and uses his beak and feet to knot them onto twigs.

He weaves in more grass, until he has made a hanging circle. He then builds the rest of the nest outward from this circle, leaving an entrance hole underneath or at the front.

The male hangs upside down from the finished nest, flapping his wings and calling to attract a female. If no female is happy with his nest, the male destroys it and starts all over again.

Social weaverbirds' nests

Social weaverbirds build their nests side by side, with one roof over all of them. There may be 30 nests under one roof, each with its own entrance underneath. Sometimes the nest is so heavy, it breaks the branches that support it.

Living in groups

Many animals live in groups instead of by themselves. The members of a group may feed together, look after each other's babies and groom each other. Groups of predators often hunt together, so they can catch bigger prey. In larger groups, the members may come and go. In smaller groups, they may stay together for longer, like a family.

These female zebras are grooming each other. They use their teeth to pick dirt, insects and bits of grass out of each other's fur.

Elephant families

Female elephants and their young live in family groups of up to 30. There is a very strong bond between the members of a family. If one elephant is injured, the others help it. If it dies, they get very upset and may stay with the body for hours. A scientist called Cynthia Moss has been studying the elephants in Amboseli National Park in Kenya since 1973. She can recognize nearly all the 650 elephants that live there and has learned a lot about how a family behaves.

Matriarch

The whole family helps to look after the babies.

The adult females are either sisters or daughters of the matriarch.

The oldest female, called the matriarch, is the leader. As she leads her family around, they learn about the area where they live.

When young females become adults, some leave to start new families.

Males leave the family when they are about 14. Adult males usually live alone.

▼ Adult female
▼ Young male
▼ Young female
▼ Baby

Fighting

Animals that live in groups are not always peaceful. Sometimes they fight each other. Pairs of males have fights over females, or to protect a particular area. In most species, the females do not fight.

Kangaroos hold each other with their front legs and kick with their back legs.

Bison put their heads together and push hard against each other.

Young giraffes use their necks to push each other slowly from side to side.

Prairie dog towns

Prairie dogs are rodents, not dogs. They get their name because they make barking noises. They live in underground burrows in family groups, called coteries. Areas where there are lots of coteries are called prairie dog towns. Today, many of these areas have been taken over by farmers, so numbers of prairie dogs are much lower than they used to be.

Adults take turns as look-outs. If there is danger, they whistle and the whole family scurries underground.

When two prairie dogs meet, they often touch noses, or "kiss", as a greeting.

Both males and females help look after the young.

Prairie dogs feed on grasses. They keep the grass around their burrows short, so they have a good view of the surrounding area.

Prairie dogs build mounds of soil around their burrow entrances. This helps stop water from getting in and flooding the burrow.

In the burrow

Inside their burrows, prairie dogs are protected from most enemies, and from the cold in winter. No two burrows are exactly the same. Like people, prairie dogs often make changes to their home. They dig new tunnels and block up old ones. A burrow may have several entrances and lots of different chambers. If it gets too crowded, some of the prairie dogs leave to dig new burrows.

Entrance

Chamber for listening for enemies above ground

Black-footed ferret chasing prairie dog down burrow

Chamber for hiding from ferrets

Rattlesnake sheltering in prairie dog burrow

Nest chamber

Chamber for sheltering when the rest of the burrow is flooded

Prairie dog digging a new tunnel

Unused tunnel blocked up with soil or droppings

Caring for young

Mammals are animals that give birth to live babies, instead of laying eggs. They feed their babies with their own milk for the first part of their lives. This is called suckling. Most newborn baby mammals cannot look after themselves. In some species, they become independent very quickly but in others, the mother looks after them for a long time. Many mammals carry their babies around when they are little.

Baboons

Baby baboons are born with black fur which turns brown as they get older. They can walk at about a week old, but their mothers carry them when they are moving far. All the members of a baboon troop help to look after the babies. They play with them and groom them.

Female olive baboon grooming her baby

Baby baboon

For its first few months, a baby baboon clings to the long hair on its mother's belly as she carries it around.

At about three months, a baby baboon can ride on its mother's back. When the mother runs, the baby lies flat and holds on tight.

Tiny kangaroos

Newborn kangaroos are only about 2.5cm (1 inch) long and weigh less than one gram (0.04oz). Immediately after being born, they climb 15cm (6 inches) to their mother's pouch, where they keep on growing.

The baby kangaroo makes its way up the front of its mother's body, pulling itself along with its front legs.

When it reaches the pouch, it crawls in and finds a nipple. It stays there feeding and growing for about six months.

Even after leaving the pouch, the baby returns to feed. It sucks from the same nipple it used when it was in the pouch.

A mother kangaroo may feed two babies at once - one tiny one inside the pouch and one bigger one outside.

Baby food

When suckling stops, baby mammals have to find food. Herbivores follow their mother around, feeding on plants when she feeds. In some species of predators, the adults feed first and then regurgitate (bring up) some of their food for their babies to eat. They do this until the babies can hunt for themselves.

Mother cheetahs sometimes catch baby gazelles and give them to their cubs so they can try out their hunting skills.

Cheetah cub chasing baby gazelle

Hiding from enemies

One of the greatest dangers for baby animals is being caught and eaten by other animals. Predators often attack babies - even those of species that they would not attack as adults. Babies are easier to catch because they are smaller and weaker and they cannot run very fast. Many animals have ways of hiding their babies from predators.

Wild dogs sometimes move their pups from one den to another so predators, such as hyenas, cannot find them so easily.

Wild dog moving pup to a new den

Pronghorns hide their fawns in long grass while they feed nearby. Fawns only spend about 20 minutes a day with their mothers.

Pronghorn fawn hiding in grass

The birth of a zebra

A female zebra lies on the ground to give birth. The baby, which is called a foal, comes out front feet first.

The birth takes about seven minutes. The mother lifts her head and licks her newborn foal to clean its fur.

Less than five minutes later, the foal tries to stand. At first, its legs are very wobbly and it keeps falling over.

When the foal has managed to stand without falling, it feeds on its mother's milk. This makes it stronger.

15 minutes after being born, the foal joins the rest of the zebra herd, ready to run with them if predators attack.

Snakes

Snakes are reptiles - animals with dry, scaly skins. The largest grassland species is the African rock python which can be up to 9m (30ft) long. All snakes are carnivores. Although they have no legs, they can move quickly to chase their prey. They usually slither along on the ground, but some species climb trees too.

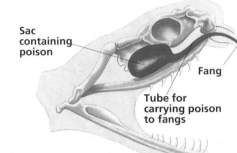

Sac containing poison

Fang

Tube for carrying poison to fangs

Many species of snakes have poison in their saliva. They have a pair of large teeth, called fangs, to inject the poison into their prey.

Boomslang snake

Weaverbird's nest

Boomslang snakes climb up acacia trees, snatch baby weaverbirds out of their nests and swallow them. They also take eggs from nests.

Weaverbird

Finding food

Snakes have poor eyesight and hearing, so they have to use other ways of finding their prey. They can feel vibrations from objects moving on the ground. They also pick up scents from the air or ground by flicking their forked tongues in and out. Some species, such as rattlesnakes, can sense tiny changes in temperature. This means they can tell if there is an animal nearby by the heat given off by its body.

Pit containing heat sensor

On each side of their heads, rattlesnakes have a small pit that contains heat sensors. These help them sense changes in temperature.

This rattlesnake has sensed the heat given off by the body of a mouse.

The mouse tries to escape, but the snake follows it into its burrow.

The snake opens its mouth wide and strikes with its poisonous fangs.

After biting the mouse, the snake lets go and waits for the poison to work.

The mouse may wander away before dying but the snake finds it again.

Open wide

Snakes do not use their teeth to tear their prey apart. Instead, they swallow it whole. Most snakes can open their mouths very wide to eat food that is much larger than their heads. They do this by unhinging their upper and lower jaws. The skin on their necks and bodies stretches easily so large food fits inside. Snakes also produce lots of saliva to help food slide down.

African egg-eating snake

Egg-eating snakes swallow whole eggs. A row of sharp spines in the snake's throat pierces the shell. The snake swallows the egg's contents and spits out the broken shell.

Rock python swallowing an impala

Rock pythons coil their bodies around their prey to suffocate it. Then they swallow it head first. It may take them hours to swallow a large animal, and days to digest it. After a big meal, the snake may not eat again for months.

Baby snakes

A few species of snakes give birth to live babies, but most lay eggs with tough, leathery shells. They lay their eggs in shallow holes, cover them with a thin layer of soil and leave them to hatch. When the baby snakes hatch out, they have to look after themselves.

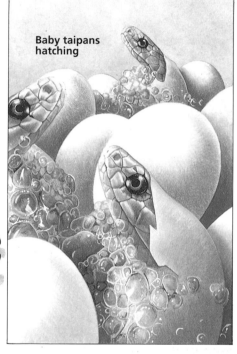

Baby taipans hatching

Warning signals

Several species of mammals and birds eat snakes. Instead of using their poison to attack an enemy immediately, many snakes give warning signals first. These may frighten the enemy into leaving them alone.

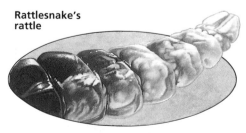

Rattlesnake's rattle

When a rattlesnake shakes the rattle at the end of its tail, it makes a loud rattling noise. The rattle is made up of interlocking sections of hard, dry skin.

As a threat, cobras raise the top part of their bodies off the ground and stretch the skin around their heads to make themselves look bigger.

Black-necked cobra

Milk snake

Coral snake

Milk snakes are harmless but they look very similar to poisonous coral snakes. Many enemies cannot tell the difference so they leave the milk snakes alone.

People in grasslands

Many groups of people live in grassland areas. For example, the Maasai people of East Africa have been living on the savanna for about 2,000 years. Today, some of them still live in small family groups and follow their traditional way of life. They keep herds of animals and get milk, meat, blood and skins from them. A Maasai group usually has two living areas, called bomas. They move from one to the other, depending on the season, so their animals always have fresh grass to eat.

The whole boma is surrounded by a fence of bushes or logs. Each family has its own entrance.

Fence

Entrance

Maasai houses are made of mud and dung, over a frame of poles. The doorways are narrow and there are no windows.

Inside the houses, it is quite dark. It is also smoky because the cooking is done on an open fire. The usual meal is a kind of milky porridge.

Each married woman lives in her own house with her children. Husbands often have more than one wife and visit them in turn.

Young animals are kept inside a small fenced area. Other animals wander freely around the boma.

The women milk the animals twice a day - once early in the morning and once in the evening. The milking takes over an hour.

Each morning, the men lead the animals out of the boma, to graze outside. They bring them in at night, so they are safe from predators.

The young men often perform exciting dances. They usually live outside the boma, only coming in for their meals.

The women fetch the firewood. They carry it on their backs and may have to walk 10km (over 6 miles) each day. They also fetch water.

This girl is dressed up for her wedding. Even on ordinary days, the women wear amazing beaded necklaces and earrings.

Farming

Today, most of the world's grasslands are used by farmers. They divide the land into fields and grow crops, such as wheat, rice and barley. They also keep animals, such as cattle, goats and sheep. Farming provides food for people, but is not always good for wild plants and animals.

Only grasses can grow well in fields where lots of farm animals feed. Other plants die if their top parts are always being eaten.

Coyote

Farmers used to kill coyotes to stop them from stealing their sheep. In some areas today, there are laws against killing coyotes.

Some of the things done by farmers are helpful to wildlife.

Wild plants have a chance to grow if farmers move their animals from field to field, leaving each field empty for part of the year.

Kori bustard waiting for insects

In Africa, farmers often burn areas of land, to grow new, green grass for their animals. Some species of birds wait at the edge of the fire, to catch insects escaping from the flames.

Danger from hunters

Many grassland animals have been hunted by people at one time or another. At first, they were hunted only by local people who depended on the animals to survive. Then outsiders moved in and began to hunt huge numbers of some species. They made money by selling skins from cheetahs, antelopes and snakes, horns from rhinos and feathers from ostriches. Some animals, such as bison and pronghorns, were hunted just for sport. Numbers got so low that some species were in danger of dying out, or becoming extinct. Today, there are laws protecting certain species but some people break the laws and go on hunting. This illegal hunting is called poaching.

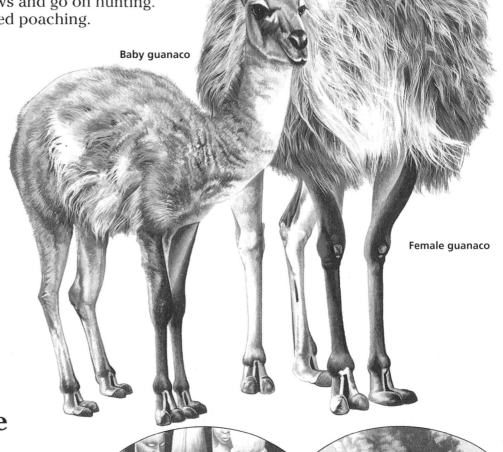

There used to be 35 million guanacos but by the beginning of this century there were only about 500,000. Today, numbers have risen to over a million, because of protection.

Baby guanaco

Female guanaco

Guanacos live in three South American countries. In Chile and Peru, they are protected but in Argentina, they are still hunted for their meat, skins and wool.

The ivory trade

Ivory comes from elephants' tusks. For thousands of years, people have been carving things from it. Since the 17th century, huge amounts of African ivory has been sold to other countries. This is called the ivory trade. Elephants are killed just so that their tusks can be pulled out and sold. In 1989, 76 countries made an agreement to stop the ivory trade, but some elephants are still killed by poachers.

Ivory is mainly used to make ornaments and bracelets. Today, many people refuse to buy ivory things. They hope that if less ivory is sold, fewer elephants will be killed.

In 1989, the president of Kenya organized a huge bonfire of tusks confiscated from poachers, to show the world that the Kenyan government was against the ivory trade.

Animal tracking

People need to know about wildlife in order to protect it. Scientists working in grassland areas can learn about how animals live by following, or tracking, them. To do this, they put the animal to sleep for a short time and fit it with a collar which has a radio transmitter on it. The scientists can then pick up signals from the transmitter, using a receiver. When the animal wakes up, its movements can be tracked from a car or plane.

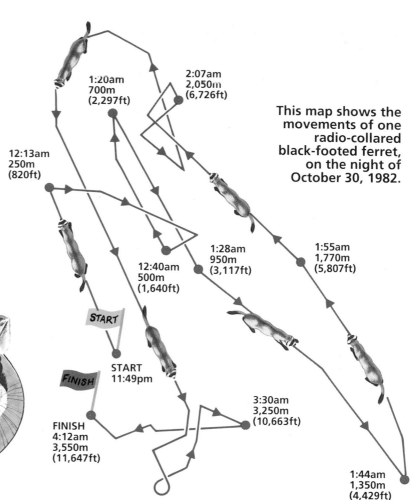

This map shows the movements of one radio-collared black-footed ferret, on the night of October 30, 1982.

1:20am
700m
(2,297ft)

2:07am
2,050m
(6,726ft)

12:13am
250m
(820ft)

2:07am
2,050m
(6,726ft)

1:28am
950m
(3,117ft)

1:55am
1,770m
(5,807ft)

12:40am
500m
(1,640ft)

START

FINISH

START
11:49pm

1:44am
1,350m
(4,429ft)

3:30am
3,250m
(10,663ft)

FINISH
4:12am
3,550m
(11,647ft)

Black-footed ferrets are almost extinct. Most surviving ferrets have been fitted with radio collars, so scientists can keep track of them.

African parks

Some African savanna areas have been made into huge parks or reserves. The animals are protected there and wardens try to stop poachers from getting in. Thousands of tourists visit these parks every year, to see the amazing wildlife. This brings money into the area and provides jobs for local people, but tourism can disturb wildlife if it is not properly controlled.

KENYA

There are over 50 parks and reserves in Kenya. They are shown in green on this map.

Cheetahs normally hunt during the day. In some areas, they have started hunting at night, so they are not disturbed by tourists in cars or vans.

Balloon rides over the savanna allow people to see the wildlife without disturbing it too much.

95

MOUNTAIN WILDLIFE

Anna Claybourne and
Antonia Cunningham

Edited by Kamini Khanduri

Scientific consultants:
Gill Standring and David Duthie

Contents

Mountains of the world

Mountains are some of the wildest places in the world. The tops of high mountains are often covered in snow, and the weather there is always cold and windy. Thick forests and steep, rocky slopes make it hard for people to live in mountain areas - but lots of different kinds of wildlife can survive there. Mountains are usually found in long lines, called ranges. The map below shows some of the world's mountain ranges.

Volcano erupting

Lava

Some mountains are volcanoes. When a volcano erupts, ash, steam and hot melted rock, called lava, burst out from under the surface of the Earth. The lava runs down the sides of the volcano.

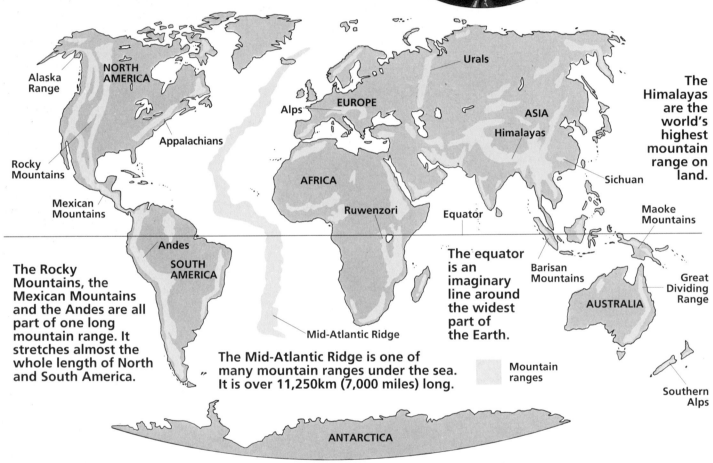

Alaska Range

NORTH AMERICA

Appalachians

Rocky Mountains

Mexican Mountains

Andes

SOUTH AMERICA

Urals

Alps

EUROPE

AFRICA

Ruwenzori

Mid-Atlantic Ridge

Equator

ASIA

Himalayas

Sichuan

The Himalayas are the world's highest mountain range on land.

Maoke Mountains

Barisan Mountains

Great Dividing Range

AUSTRALIA

Southern Alps

ANTARCTICA

The Rocky Mountains, the Mexican Mountains and the Andes are all part of one long mountain range. It stretches almost the whole length of North and South America.

The Mid-Atlantic Ridge is one of many mountain ranges under the sea. It is over 11,250km (7,000 miles) long.

The equator is an imaginary line around the widest part of the Earth.

Mountain ranges

Mountain sizes

These pictures show the different heights of some mountains around the world.

Everest, Himalayas
8,846m (29,022ft)

K2, Himalayas
8,611m (28,251ft)

McKinley, Alaska Range
6,194m (20,321ft)

Kilimanjaro, Africa
5,895m (19,340ft)

Aconcagua, Andes
6,960m (22,834ft)

Mont Blanc, Alps
4,807m (15,771ft)

Fujiyama, Japan
3,776m (12,389ft)

In the mountains

There are many kinds, or species, of plants and animals living in the mountains. The type of place where an animal or plant lives is called its habitat. Different mountain species live in different mountain habitats. Not many species live near the top of a high mountain because of the harsh weather. Lower down, where it is warmer and more sheltered, there is more wildlife. These pictures show the different levels on a mountain in North America, and some of the wildlife that lives there.

Some species of birds fly near the tops of mountains. They are mostly large birds that can fly in strong winds.

Golden eagle

The top of a mountain is called a peak. Many mountains have snow on their peaks all year long. The level where the snow ends is called the snowline.

Mountain goats and sheep live on the rocky slopes during summer. They can climb steep mountainsides and leap from rock to rock.

Rocky Mountain goat

Below the snowy mountain tops, there are often steep slopes covered with rocks and loose stones.

Many bright flowers grow on the grassy slopes. Insects, such as bees and butterflies, fly among the flowers.

Apollo butterfly

Purple saxifrage

Below the rocky slopes, there are grassy meadows where small plants grow. Many animals live here.

Mountain forests are home to many different kinds of wildlife, such as cougars, wolverines and porcupines.

Cougar

It is too cold and windy for trees to grow high up on mountains. The level where trees start growing is called the treeline.

Beyond the trees

It can be hard for animals and plants to survive high up in the mountains. There are hardly any trees to give shelter, it is very windy and the ground is rocky and hard to cross. When the sun shines, it can get very hot, but at night the temperature drops below freezing point. Over millions of years, mountain animals and plants have gradually become well-suited to living in these harsh surroundings. This is called adaptation.

Rock climbers

Ibexes spend most of the year in rocky areas high up in the mountains. They can climb incredibly steep slopes and jump from rock to rock, leaping over huge gaps. They eat tough grasses and other small plants that grow among the rocks. Sometimes it is hard to find enough to eat above the treeline, but ibexes can go without food for several days while they look for more.

Ibex

Male ibexes show off their strength during the mating season by standing up on their back legs. They also fight over females, attacking each other with their long horns.

Ibexes have hooves with narrow edges that dig into cracks in the rocks, and slightly hollow soles that help them cling to rocky slopes. They have two toes which spread out when they land, making it easier for them to balance.

Goats and sheep

These goats and sheep are found in different countries but they all live in similar ways. They spend part of the year above the treeline. Their horns get bigger as the animals get older.

Mouflon   Markhor   Bighorn sheep   Tahr   Chamois   Rocky Mountain goat

Surviving the winter

Life is even harder for mountain animals in the winter. It is freezing cold, snow covers the ground and there is little food to be found. Many animals have very thick coats to keep them warm. Some also shelter inside a den or burrow.

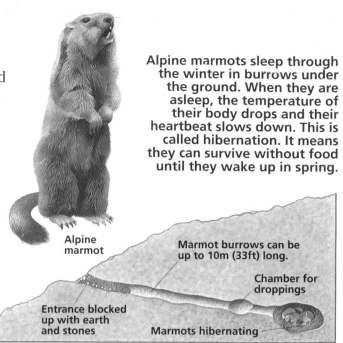

Alpine marmots sleep through the winter in burrows under the ground. When they are asleep, the temperature of their body drops and their heartbeat slows down. This is called hibernation. It means they can survive without food until they wake up in spring.

Alpine marmot

Snow leopards live high up in the mountains of Asia. They have thick fur all over their bodies, even on the soles of their feet. Snow leopards shelter in dens between rocks, but often come out to find food.

Marmot burrows can be up to 10m (33ft) long.

Chamber for droppings

Entrance blocked up with earth and stones

Marmots hibernating

Making hay

Pikas are small animals that live on rocky slopes high up in the mountains of North America and Asia. In the winter, they feed on dried plants, or hay, that they have stored up the summer before.

During the summer, a pika collects grass and other plants to store for the winter. It is easier to find food in warm weather.

The pika carries bundles of plants to a rock and lays them out to dry. Dried plants, or hay, keep longer than fresh ones.

The pika guards its food while it dries, because other pikas may try to steal it. It sniffs the air, and lifts its head to look around.

Moving away

In the winter, red deer move down the mountain to live in the forests until spring. The male deer, called stags, go down first. Large groups of females, called hinds, follow a few weeks later. They travel in long lines of up to 500 animals.

Male deer have large horns, called antlers. These drop off every spring. It takes about three months for a new pair to grow.

Red deer stag

Red deer hinds moving down the mountain

Yaks

Yaks are huge, hairy relatives of cows. They live high up in the mountains of Asia and eat grass and other plants. Their thick coats help protect them from the freezing cold, but they also have another good way of keeping warm. Their stomachs give out heat when they digest, or break down, food. This warms the yaks' bodies from the inside.

Yaks have long, shaggy coats that almost touch the ground. Their horns start growing when they are about two years old.

Female yak

In Nepal and Tibet, people keep yaks as farm animals. They use them for carrying heavy loads up and down mountainsides. They also get milk and butter from them.

Baby yaks are called calves. Yaks usually have only one calf at a time.

Yak calf

Mosses and lichens

On high mountain slopes, the soil is thin and stony. Above the grassy meadows, there are not many plants. Only mosses and lichens can survive very high up. They usually grow on rocks close to the ground, where it is less windy.

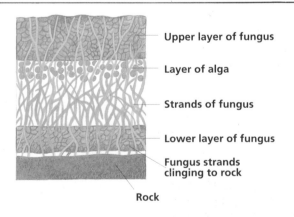

Upper layer of fungus

Layer of alga

Strands of fungus

Lower layer of fungus

Fungus strands clinging to rock

Rock

Mosses

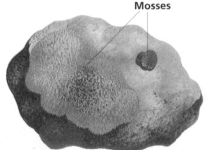

Lichens

The picture above shows how lichens are made up of an alga and a fungus living together. The fungus surrounds the alga and helps it to stay moist. The alga makes food for itself and for the fungus.

Tails for jumping

Springtails are tiny insects. They live in shallow soil and feed on dead plants. They can survive cold weather because they have a chemical in their bodies which stops them from freezing. They use their strong tails to jump short distances.

Tail

When a springtail is crawling around or standing still, its tail is folded under its body.

When it wants to jump, it flicks its tail down onto the ground very quickly and suddenly.

By pushing its tail against the ground, the springtail jumps up into the air.

Small mammals

These pictures show three small mammals that live above the treeline. Mammals are animals that give birth to live young instead of laying eggs. Baby mammals feed on their mother's milk. All mammals need to keep warm, but small mammals lose heat from their bodies more quickly than larger ones. They need very thick fur to keep out the cold.

Chinchillas live in South America. They have very thick, soft fur, with up to 60 hairs growing out of each tiny hole, or pore, in their skin. Most mammals have only one hair in each pore.

Chinchilla

Mountain viscacha

Mountain viscachas live in South America. They sleep in cracks between rocks. During the day, they often sit in the sunshine to keep warm.

Hoary marmots live in North America. They dig underground burrows, where they sleep at night. They also use their burrows as hiding places if they are in danger.

Hoary marmot

Birds of prey

Birds of prey, such as falcons, eagles and hawks, feed on other birds or on small mammals. Many species live above the treeline. They often build nests on rocks, or in shallow holes in the ground. Sometimes they use another bird's old nest. Birds of prey have very good eyesight. Most hunt during the day, so they can see their prey from far away.

Gyrfalcon feeding on a pigeon

Gyrfalcons fly near the ground to chase their prey. Then they grab it with their large claws and tear it apart with their strong beaks.

103

Forests in the north

In the most northern parts of the world, the summers are very short and the winters are very long and freezing cold. Only trees such as firs, spruces and pines can grow on the mountains there. These types of trees are called conifers. Many animals move down to the conifer forests in the autumn, because the trees provide food and shelter during the winter. This picture shows part of a conifer forest high in the Rocky Mountains in North America.

Goshawks hunt small animals, including other birds.

Goshawk

Bluebird

Conifers

Conifers are well adapted to cold weather. Their needles are tougher than ordinary flat leaves, so they can keep growing in winter. Conifer seeds are hidden inside a hard cone.

Cone cut in half

Hard scales

Seed

Conifer trees are shaped so that snow can slide off their branches.

Every winter, snowshoe hares grow an extra-thick coat of white fur to keep them warm.

Snowshoe hare

Red crossbills use the crossed tips of their beaks to break into cones and reach the seeds inside.

Red crossbill

Wapiti

Wapiti are a kind of deer. They eat small plants, tree bark and leaves. Every year, each male's antlers fall off and another pair grows.

Spruce grouse eat pine needles.

Woodpeckers peck holes in tree trunks to find insects.

Hairy woodpecker

Wolverine

Wolverines eat other animals, such as hares and young deer.

Mushrooms, mosses and lichens grow on the dry, cold ground under the snow.

Chanterelle mushrooms

In winter, porcupines eat pine needles and tree bark. They shelter between tree roots or in hollow logs.

North American porcupine

Animal tracks can be seen in the snow.

Wolverine tracks

The mating season

Wapiti spend the summer above the treeline, and the winter in conifer forests. Male and female wapiti usually live in separate groups. They mate every year in September. Their mating season is called the rut.

At the start of the rut, a stag (male wapiti) gets restless. He leaves his group and goes off on his own.

The stag goes to look for some hinds (females). He roars very loudly to let other stags know he is there and to show off his strength.

The stag thrashes his antlers against the trees. He rounds up a large group of hinds to mate with.

He fights other stags that try to take his hinds, locking his antlers with theirs in a test of strength. The winner stays with the hinds.

Mountain rainforests

Near the equator, the weather is usually hot and damp. Thick, wet forests, called rainforests, grow there. They are home to thousands of different kinds of animals and plants. Rainforests that grow on mountain slopes often have their own wildlife species. The map below shows the mountain rainforest areas of the world.

Mountain anoa

EUROPE
ASIA
AFRICA
NORTH AMERICA
Equator
SOUTH AMERICA
AUSTRALIA

Mountain rainforest areas

Mountain anoas only live on one island, called Sulawesi, in Southeast Asia. They are so rare that scientists have found out very little about them.

Leopards live in many different habitats in Africa and Asia, including mountain rainforests. They eat animals such as lizards, birds, deer and monkeys. They are good at climbing and sometimes drag their prey up into trees to eat it.

Leopards feeding

Chameleons

Jackson's chameleons live in African mountain rainforests. They creep slowly along branches to hunt for insects.

A chameleon can keep its body still and swivel its huge eyes around in different directions, to look for prey.

If it sees an insect, such as a fly, the chameleon suddenly shoots out its long, sticky tongue to catch it.

The fly sticks to the end of the chameleon's tongue. Then the chameleon pulls its tongue back into its mouth and eats the fly.

Apes and monkeys

There are many different kinds of apes and monkeys living in the mountain rainforests of Asia, Africa and South America. Apes, such as gorillas and chimpanzees, have no tails. Monkeys have tails, and are usually smaller than apes. Several monkey species have very strong tails which they use like an extra arm, for holding onto branches. These are called prehensile tails.

De Brazza's guenon

Hanuman langur

Black and white colobus monkey

Woolly monkey

Stump-tailed macaque

Spider monkey's tail   Rubbery skin

The prehensile tails of some monkey species have no fur on the underside. The skin is hard and rubbery, with ridges. This helps the monkey to grip onto branches.

Prehensile tail

Spider monkey

Owl-faced monkey

Chimpanzees

Francois's langur

Mountain gorilla

Mountains of the Moon

The Ruwenzori mountains in Africa are sometimes called the Mountains of the Moon. Rainforests grow on their lower slopes but higher up, there are strange forests of giant flowers. Some species of groundsel and lobelia grow up to 9m (30ft) high in the Ruwenzori. In most other places, these types of plants only grow to about 0.6m (2ft) high.

Giant lobelia

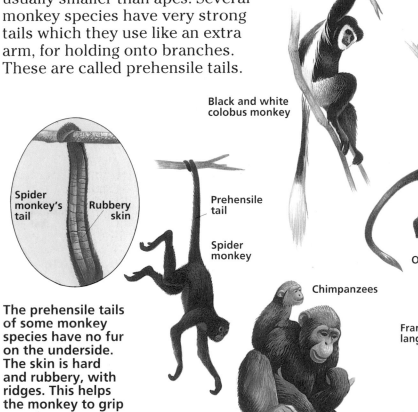

Giant groundsel

Giant earthworms live in the soil near rivers in the Ruwenzori mountains. They can grow to 75cm (2.5ft) long.

Water wildlife

When rain falls on the mountains, it runs into small, fast-flowing streams. These rush down the mountainsides and join together to become rivers. Cold, clear mountain lakes form in the valleys between the slopes. Many different wildlife species live in and around streams, rivers and lakes. The picture on these pages shows a mountain stream in Europe, and some of the wildlife that lives there.

Tiny plants, called algae, float in water. They are a source of food for some water animals. Algae are so small they can only be seen with a microscope.

Algae

Insects

Many insects live near mountain streams. Some of them lay their eggs in the water. When the young insects hatch, they live in the water until they are almost fully grown. Then they climb out and turn into adults by shedding their skins.

Young insects are called larvae or nymphs. They often look very different from the adults.

Stonefly nymph

Mayfly nymph

Adult mayfly

Adult stonefly

Adult caddis fly

Some caddis fly larvae use tiny stones or twigs to build a hard case around their bodies. This protects them from enemies and stops them from being swept away.

Caddis fly larva

Waterfall

There are often lots of plants near waterfalls. The splashing water makes the ground damp, so it is easy for them to grow there.

Dipper

Dippers often stand on stones in streams.

Otters

Otters live in burrows, called holts, near streams and rivers. They often swim underwater to catch fish.

Dippers

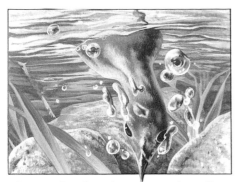

Dippers feed on insects and snails that live on the stream bed. They run down the side of a rock into the water, or dive in head first, with their eyes open.

Once they are underwater, dippers spread their wings to keep their balance in the fast-flowing stream. They walk along the bottom, looking for food among the stones.

If a dipper finds an insect or a snail, it catches it in its beak. It quickly hops out of the water and stands on a rock to eat its food. Then it goes underwater again.

Many animals come to mountain streams to drink.

Red deer

Water moss grows on rocks. It can live above and below the water surface.

Water moss

Underwater life

In mountain streams, the water flows very quickly. Large fish are strong enough to swim against the flow, but small ones have to cling to rocks or hide under stones to avoid being swept away. Fish also live in mountain lakes, where the water does not move very fast.

Bullheads lie on the stony stream bed. The water flows more slowly there, so they do not get swept away. Their spotted skin helps them blend in with their surroundings.

Bullhead on the stream bed

Stone loaches

Stone loaches cling to rocks with their mouths to stop themselves from being swept away.

Crayfish live under stones in streams and rivers. In spite of their name, they are not fish, but are related to crabs and lobsters.

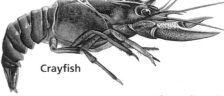

Crayfish

Charr

Charr live in high mountain lakes. The males have very bright markings.

Amazing journeys

Salmon lay their eggs in mountain streams. The newly hatched salmon stay in the stream for up to six years, then swim down to the sea. A few years later, they return to their home stream to lay their eggs. The pictures below show Atlantic salmon.

The salmon leave the sea and swim up the river that leads to their home stream. Scientists think they may find their way partly by the smell and taste of the water.

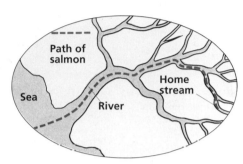

The salmon have to be very strong to survive the long journey upstream. They do not eat anything on the way. Some of them become exhausted and die on the journey.

During the journey, the salmon leap over waterfalls and rocks. They can jump as high as 3m (10ft) in the air, using their tails to push themselves out of the water.

When the salmon arrive at their home streams, each female flaps her tail on the stream bed to make a hollow, called a redd. She lays up to 15,000 eggs in it.

When the baby salmon, called fry, hatch out, they feed on the yolks of their eggs, which are still attached to them. Later, the yolks drop off and the fry feed on insects.

Fishing for salmon

In Alaska in North America, brown bears fish for Pacific salmon which swim up mountain rivers to breed. For most of the year, bears eat leaves, berries, honey and insects and other animals. When they get the chance to eat salmon, they eat as much as possible. The bears catch fish in several different ways.

Bears learn to fish when they are very young.

Some bears snap up the fish in their jaws.

Some bears use their paws to flip the fish out of the water and into their mouths.

Some bears dive into the water, pin the fish to the river bed with their paws, and then grab them with their teeth.

Flamingos in the Andes

High in the Andes mountains in South America, there are large, shallow lakes which are home to big groups of flamingos. The flamingos feed on tiny plants and animals that live in the water and in the mud at the bottom of the lakes.

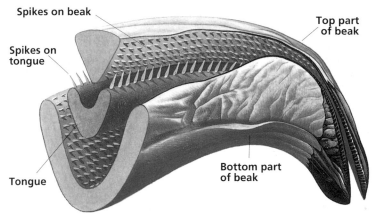

Spikes on beak

Spikes on tongue

Top part of beak

Tongue

Bottom part of beak

Flamingos feed with their heads upside-down. They stick their beaks into the mud, and suck in a mixture of water, mud and food.

The picture above shows part of a flamingo's beak. When a flamingo feeds, food sticks to small spikes on the inside of its beak. The flamingo quickly scrapes the food off, using larger spikes on its tongue. Then it swallows the food and pushes the water and mud back out of its beak.

Mountain monkeys

Japanese macaques are a species of monkey. They are sometimes called snow monkeys. They live in Japan in mountain forests and on rocky slopes. Macaques spend a lot of time playing and swimming in rivers and streams. In some parts of Japan, there are places called hot springs, where warm water comes out of the ground. The macaques sit in the hot water during the winter, to keep warm.

Sometimes, macaques spend nearly all day sitting in the hot springs. When it is very cold, snow may fall and settle on their heads. Macaques often sit in the hot water right up to their necks.

Acid lakes

The water in mountain lakes is not always clean. If there is pollution in the air, this may fall into lakes as acid rain or snow (see page 127). Fish cannot live in polluted water. Other animals may also die if there are not enough fish for them to eat.

Acid lakes often look clean, but very little wildlife can survive there.

Hunting and escaping

In every habitat, there are predators - animals that hunt other animals for food. The animals that they hunt are called prey. In mountain areas there are lots of species of predators, such as bears, wolves, birds of prey and big cats. Different predators hunt in different ways and prey animals have lots of different ways of trying to escape. One way of showing which animals eat what is by a food web. The picture below shows part of a food web in a North American mountain habitat. (The pictures are not to scale.)

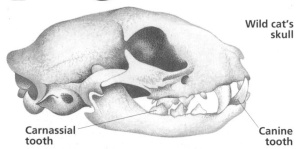

Wild cat's skull

Carnassial tooth

Canine tooth

Like many predators, wild cats have teeth that are well-suited to eating meat. They have long canine teeth for biting and killing, and sharp carnassial teeth for slicing and chewing.

The arrows point from the plant or animal that is eaten to the animal that eats it. For example, mayfly nymphs are eaten by salmon, and salmon are eaten by brown bears.

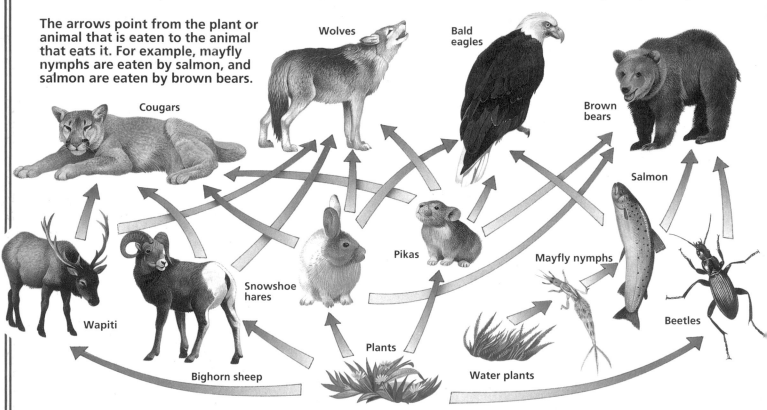

Cougars

Wolves

Bald eagles

Brown bears

Salmon

Wapiti

Snowshoe hares

Pikas

Mayfly nymphs

Beetles

Bighorn sheep

Plants

Water plants

Hunting in groups

Wolves live in mountain forests in many parts of Asia and North America. They live in groups, called packs. A wolf cannot kill big animals on its own, so the wolves in a pack often go hunting together.

These wolves have smelled a deer somewhere nearby. They can tell exactly where the deer is by picking up its scent.

The wolves approach the deer in a long line, with the wind blowing in their direction so the deer cannot smell them.

When the deer sees the wolves, it starts running. The wolves chase after it and surround it, cutting off its escape route.

If the wolves catch the deer, they attack it, drag it to the ground and kill it. Then they eat it as quickly as possible.

Territories

Many predators mark out an area of land for themselves, by leaving droppings and scratching on trees with their claws. This area is called a territory. Each animal hunts in its own territory, so there are not too many predators of the same species competing for the same prey. Males do not usually go into each other's territories.

This map shows the territories of two male bobcats and three females.

Each female bobcat has a den in her territory, where she gives birth to her kittens.

Male and female bobcats have overlapping territories, so they can mate with each other.

Male bobcats fight if they meet in the small area where their territories overlap.

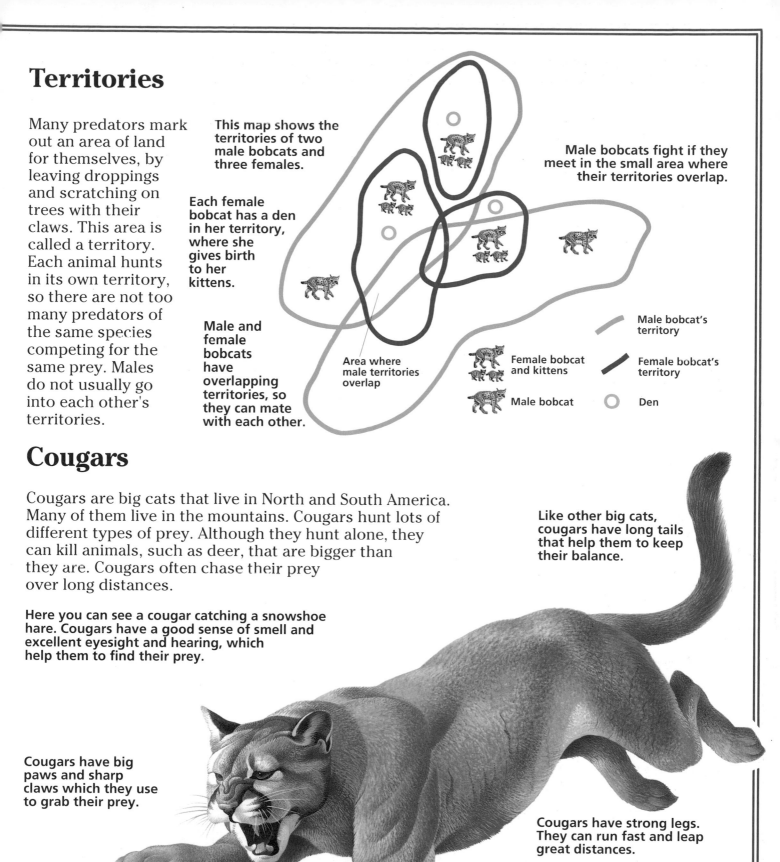

Area where male territories overlap

Female bobcat and kittens	Male bobcat's territory
Male bobcat	Female bobcat's territory
	Den

Cougars

Cougars are big cats that live in North and South America. Many of them live in the mountains. Cougars hunt lots of different types of prey. Although they hunt alone, they can kill animals, such as deer, that are bigger than they are. Cougars often chase their prey over long distances.

Like other big cats, cougars have long tails that help them to keep their balance.

Here you can see a cougar catching a snowshoe hare. Cougars have a good sense of smell and excellent eyesight and hearing, which help them to find their prey.

Cougars have big paws and sharp claws which they use to grab their prey.

Cougars have strong legs. They can run fast and leap great distances.

Avoiding predators

Animals that are hunted by other animals do not always get caught. They escape by running away, hiding or fighting back at their enemies. Some animals, though, have more unusual ways of avoiding being eaten.

Snowshoe hares are hunted by many kinds of predators. They are specially adapted to spotting predators and running away fast.

Big ears to listen for predators

Good eyesight to spot approaching predators

Strong back legs help hares to run and jump fast.

Hairs on soles of feet give extra grip on slippery ground.

Snowshoe hares have big, flat back feet which help to stop them from sinking in soft snow.

These pictures show how a hare leaps along.

The hare leaps forward, taking off from its back feet.

It lands on its front feet.

Then it puts its back feet down in front, and leaps again.

Camouflage

Many animals match their surroundings, so predators cannot see them so easily. This is called camouflage. Some mountain animals also change their appearance with the seasons, so they can blend with different backgrounds at different times of the year.

Common green grasshoppers are well-camouflaged on the grassy meadows where they live.

Ptarmigan in summer

Ptarmigan in winter

Ptarmigans grow white feathers in winter, to blend with the snow, and speckled brown feathers in summer, to blend with the rocks and plants.

Porcupines

If porcupines are attacked, they defend themselves in an unusual way. They are covered with sharp spines, or quills, which come away from the porcupine's skin if they are touched.

When there is no danger, a porcupine's quills lie flat against its body, pointing in the same direction as its tail.

When the porcupine sees a predator, such as a cougar, its quills stand on end, or bristle, and point in all directions. This frightens most predators away.

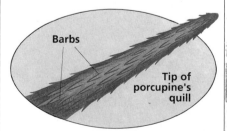

Barbs

Tip of porcupine's quill

If a predator does attack, some of the porcupine's quills may stick into it. Each quill has tiny spikes, called barbs, on its tip. These dig into the predator's skin and make it very painful to pull the quill out again.

Playing tricks

Some animals use tricks to avoid being eaten. Some species pretend to be dead if they see a predator. Most predators only eat prey they have killed themselves, so they leave the animal alone. Other species have markings that make them look like more dangerous animals. This often frightens predators away.

Ringed snakes live on boggy hillsides in Europe. When a predator is nearby, they pretend to be dead. They lie coiled up with their heads upside-down and their tongues hanging out.

Emperor moths have two spots on their wings that look like a large pair of eyes. Birds that eat moths are frightened away, because the moth looks like the face of a much bigger animal.

Safety in numbers

Animals are often safer from predators if they live in groups. The members of a group can warn each other if there is danger. In some species, one animal gives a warning call if it sees a predator approaching. This gives the rest of the group a chance to hide.

In the African mountains, groups of rock hyraxes often lie together in the sun. If one hyrax sees a predator, such as a snake or an eagle, it makes a loud screaming call to warn all the others.

Hyrax making a warning call

Mountain birds

Hundreds of species of birds live in mountain areas. Big birds of prey, such as eagles, often live high up on rocky slopes. They can fly in strong winds without being blown away. Smaller birds usually live in the meadows and forests lower down. In the winter, many mountain birds move away to warmer areas. Some fly incredibly long distances, often to other countries. These journeys are called migrations. These pictures show some birds that spend the summer in mountains in different parts of Europe.

Grey wagtail

Alpine swift

Dotterel

Wood warbler

Crag martin

Red-throated pipit

Snow bunting

Alpine accentor

House martin

Siskin

Redpoll

Greenshank

Rock thrush

Wheatear

Bluethroat

Ring ouzel

Staying all winter

Some birds stay in the mountains all year long. Wallcreepers spend the summer high up among the rocks and snow, and move a little lower down the mountain for the winter. Snow finches usually stay high up all winter, and only move down the mountain if the weather is extremely cold.

Wallcreepers grip the sides of cliffs with their large claws, and use their long beaks to search for insects in cracks between the rocks.

Snow finches feeding

Snow finch fluffing out its feathers

Wallcreeper

Snow finches feed in large flocks. In winter, they often go into mountain towns and villages, where people may feed them. They fluff out their feathers to keep warm.

Showing off

The males of some bird species dance and show off their bright markings to attract females. These performances are called courtship displays. Temminck's tragopans, which live in Chinese mountain forests, perform amazing displays.

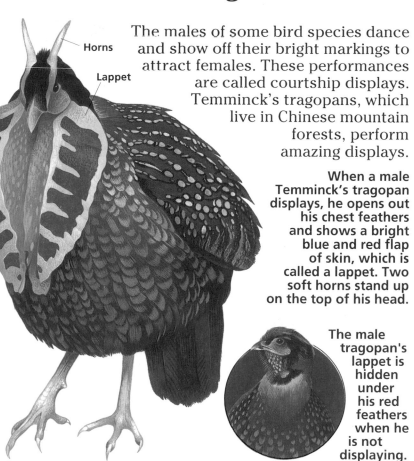

Horns

Lappet

When a male Temminck's tragopan displays, he opens out his chest feathers and shows a bright blue and red flap of skin, which is called a lappet. Two soft horns stand up on the top of his head.

The male tragopan's lappet is hidden under his red feathers when he is not displaying.

Group displays

Black grouse live in forests and meadows on mountains in Europe. The males perform noisy courtship displays in a group. The area where they display is called a lek. Female black grouse, called greyhens, come to the lek to watch the males.

This picture shows a black grouse lek. The males call loudly and display in several different positions. The positions have different names.

Greyhens watching the display

Crowing display position

Upright display position

Rookooing display position

Building a nest

Birds need somewhere safe to lay their eggs. In forests, most birds build nests in trees. Above the treeline, it is harder to find good nesting places. Like other animals, mountain birds have become adapted to their surroundings. They nest in different ways, depending on their habitat.

Anna's hummingbirds live in mountain forests. The female uses lichens and plants to build a tiny nest in a tree. She ties the nest onto a branch with spider's webs, to stop it from being blown away.

Ptarmigans live mainly above the treeline. They make their nests on the ground, in a hollow lined with grass and feathers. The nest is often hidden among rocks or bushes, so predators cannot easily see it.

Peregrine falcons do not build nests at all. They lay their eggs on high rocky ledges. Most other animals cannot reach these ledges, so the falcon eggs and chicks are safe there.

Golden eagles

Golden eagles are large, powerful birds of prey that are found in mountains in many parts of the world. They have big, sharp claws, called talons, which they use for catching their prey. They eat hares, marmots and other small mammals, and sometimes catch larger animals, such as young chamois. Golden eagles live in pairs and usually build their nests, called eyries, high up on rocky ledges.

The male eagle goes hunting and brings back food for the chicks.

The female eagle tears up meat for the chicks until they have learned how to feed themselves.

Golden eagle chicks

An eyrie is made of sticks and branches, and lined with dry mosses and grass.

Growing up

Golden eagles usually have two eggs at a time. The female guards the eggs, which take about six weeks to hatch.

One of the young chicks is bigger than the other. The two chicks fight each other, and the smaller one usually dies.

The chick that survives starts to grow brown feathers, called flight feathers, when it is four or five weeks old.

A few months later, the young eagle is big and strong enough to fly away. It leaves the nest to live on its own.

High fliers

Bar-headed geese breed in central Asia in the summer, and migrate over the Himalayas every year to spend the winter in northern India. They have been known to fly as high as 10,000m (33,000ft) - higher than Mount Everest.

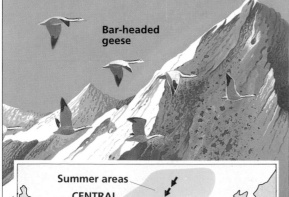

Bar-headed geese

Summer areas
CENTRAL ASIA
Himalayas
Winter areas
INDIA
Migration routes
←←←←

Scavengers

Sometimes, meat-eaters feed on animals that have already died, instead of killing them themselves. This is called scavenging. Lots of mountain birds are scavengers. They eat animals that have fallen on the rocks.

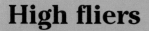

Lammergeier

Lammergeiers eat the marrow from inside animal bones. They sometimes carry bones up into the sky and drop them onto the rocks below to break them open.

Griffon vulture scavenging

Griffon vultures eat as much as they can, in case they do not find any more food for a while. They often eat so much that they are too full to fly away immediately.

Amazing birds of the Andes

The Andes mountains in South America are home to some of the world's largest and smallest birds. Huge Andean condors fly among the mountain peaks, and tiny hummingbirds live in the meadows and forests lower down.

Andean condor

Sparkling violetear hummingbird

Sparkling violetear hummingbirds are about 13cm (5in) long. They use their long beaks to suck a sweet liquid, called nectar, out of flowers.

Andean condors are the biggest birds of prey in the world. They can weigh up to 12.5kg (27lb) and measure over 120cm (47in) from the tips of their beaks to the ends of their tails.

Andean condor

Sparkling violetear hummingbird

Andean condors are almost a thousand times heavier than sparkling violetear hummingbirds.

The mountains of China

In the mountainous Sichuan area of central China, the weather is always damp and misty. Thick forests of trees and bamboo plants grow on the steep slopes. These forests are home to many rare animal species, such as pandas and golden monkeys.

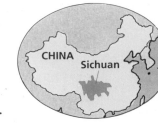

Giant pandas

Giant pandas are rare relatives of bears. There are only about 700 of them left in the wild. They live mainly in Sichuan in the cool, damp forests, feeding on bamboo stems and leaves. They also eat other kinds of plants, small mammals, birds, fish and eggs. Giant pandas do not hibernate, but when it is very cold, they shelter in caves or hollow trees.

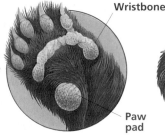

Wristbone

Paw pad

Giant pandas have five fingers on each front paw. They also have an extra large wristbone, which they use like a thumb to grip bamboo while they are eating it.

Giant pandas

Giant pandas mate in spring. When a female is ready to mate, she bleats and leaves her scent on trees to attract a male.

When a male panda is attracted, he answers her with high-pitched calls. The two pandas play together before they mate.

About five months later, the female makes a den in a cave, where she gives birth to one or two tiny, blind cubs.

The mother only cares for one of the cubs, so the other one dies. The cub that survives starts to grow fur after about ten days.

Young giant pandas are very playful. They often roll on their backs while they feed. They stay with their mothers for about 18 months.

Bamboo

When bamboo plants flower, the stems and leaves die, so giant pandas cannot always find enough to eat. For example, in Sichuan in 1983, a large area of bamboo flowered and died. Many giant pandas died as a result.

Giant pandas have two different kinds of teeth. They use their sharp front teeth for biting, and their hard, flat back teeth for chewing bamboo.

Sichuan species

Here are some of the other animals that live in the mountains of Sichuan.

Golden monkeys live in forests where there are lots of oak and chestnut trees. The fur on their backs can be up to 10cm (4in) long.

Golden monkey

Takins have long, shaggy coats. They live in bamboo forests and give out a strong, oily smell from all over their bodies.

Takin

Red pandas are distant relatives of giant pandas. They usually come out at night to eat fruit, roots, bamboo and other plants. Scientists think they may eat meat too.

Red panda

Musk deer

Small, shy musk deer live in forests. They eat grass, leaves, mosses and lichens. The males have long, sharp front teeth, which they use for fighting other males.

Pheasants

There are about 50 species of pheasants in the world. Many of these come from Sichuan. The pheasants shown here live in forests near the treeline. Males usually have brighter feathers than females.

Brown eared pheasant

Lady Amherst's pheasant

Common pheasant

Blood pheasant

Reeve's pheasant

Chinese Monal pheasant

Golden pheasant

Spring in the Alps

The Alps are a big range of mountains in Europe. During winter, they are almost completely covered in snow. When spring begins, some of the snow melts. As sunshine warms the damp ground, small plants start growing. Animals that have been asleep all winter come out of their burrows to find food. Other animals, such as chamois, come up from the forests to the meadows and rocky slopes that were covered in snow in winter. Many animals give birth in spring. It is easier for their babies to find food and keep warm at this time of year.

In warmer weather, the snow lower down the mountain melts. This means that the snowline is higher up in spring than it is in winter.

Snowline in spring

Snowline in winter

Young golden eagle

Golden eagles and other birds of prey fly high in the sky, looking for small mammals on the ground.

Alpine choughs can live very high up in the Alps. They eat insects and seeds.

Alpine chough

Female chamois and their babies, called kids, live together in herds. Kids stay with their mothers for about two years.

Herd of chamois

Female chamois

Chamois kid

In spring, mountain hares have a mixture of brown and white fur. Their white winter coats are gradually turning brown for the summer, so that the hares will be camouflaged among rocks and plants.

Mountain hare

Insects, such as butterflies and bees, fly close to the ground, feeding on nectar from flowers.

Alpine salamanders eat insects and slugs. They hide under stones, only coming out after showers of rain.

Honeybee

Spotted fritillary butterfly

Small Apollo butterfly

Alpine salamander

Swallowtail butterfly

Spotted fritillaries

Spotted fritillary butterflies pair up and mate in spring. Then the female lays her eggs on a small plant.

After a few days, caterpillars hatch out of the eggs. During the summer, they feed on the leaves of the plant.

In the autumn, each caterpillar grows a hard outer covering, called a pupa. This protects it during the harsh winter.

Inside the pupa, the caterpillar slowly changes into a butterfly. In spring, the butterfly comes out and looks for a mate.

Alpine marmots

Marmots come out of their burrows to look for plants to eat.

Gentian

Yellow mountain saxifrage

Spring flowers

Many mountain plants flower in spring. They grow mainly in the meadows and among the rocks. Some plants are very rare, so there are laws to stop people from picking them. They are called protected plants. These pictures show some of the flowers that grow in the Alps in spring.

Gentian

Edelweiss

Rock soapwort

Bear's-ear

Alpine aster

Yellow mountain saxifrage

Purple saxifrage

Mountain buttercup

Mountain avens

Alpine soldanellas

Alpine soldanellas can grow above the snowline. They give out heat as they grow. This melts the snow so the flowers can come through.

123

People in the mountains

Most mountain people live in tiny villages, far away from cities and towns. Many of them are farmers. They keep herds of animals and grow crops on the steep slopes. Life in a high mountain village can be very hard. The weather is often extremely cold, and above the treeline there are no trees for firewood. It is difficult to grow crops because the soil is thin and stony and is easily washed down the mountainside by the rain.

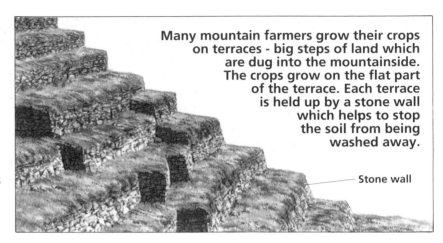

Many mountain farmers grow their crops on terraces - big steps of land which are dug into the mountainside. The crops grow on the flat part of the terrace. Each terrace is held up by a stone wall which helps to stop the soil from being washed away.

Stone wall

Sherpas

The Sherpas live in villages in the Himalayas, the highest mountains in the world. Most Sherpas live in Nepal. They grow rice and potatoes on their farms, and keep yaks as farm animals. They make butter and cheese out of yak milk, and use yak skin and wool to make clothes. Yak dung (droppings) is used instead of firewood.

Temple

There is a temple in every village. Most people pray there every day.

Sherpa houses are usually made of stone, with very thick walls to keep out the cold. The animals live in stables downstairs, and the people live upstairs. The warmth from the animals' bodies helps to heat the house.

Rooms upstairs for people

Stables downstairs for animals

Yak

During the day, the yaks wander around, feeding on grass. They are put back into their stables at night.

Sherpa children often have to help their parents by doing farm work, but today, most of them go to school as well. They sometimes have their lessons outside.

Many Sherpas work as guides, or porters, for tourists and climbers. They show people the safest paths to use in the mountains, and help them carry their heavy bags.

Mountain climbing

People climb mountains as a sport, or to see the wildlife there. A climb to the top of a mountain is called an ascent. In 1953, Edmund Hillary, a climber from New Zealand, and Tenzing Norgay, a Sherpa porter, made the first ascent of Everest. They were with a group of climbers, but only Hillary and Tenzing got to the top.

This picture shows the route Hillary and Tenzing took.

╱ Hillary and Tenzing's route

▲ Camp

FINISH

Mount Everest

For their ascent, Hillary and Tenzing wore special boots to stop them from slipping. They took ice axes, for climbing on ice, and oxygen, to help them breathe.

The ascent took several weeks, so the climbers had to stop at camps on the way.

The base camp was the starting point for the ascent.

START

Base camp

Abominable snowmen

Many people believe that a strange kind of animal, called the Yeti, lives in the Himalayas. It is sometimes called the abominable snowman. Lots of big footprints have been found, but nobody has ever caught a Yeti or found a dead one. In North America, people believe in a similar creature, which they call Bigfoot.

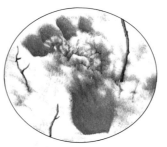

Lots of people have seen footprints like this one. They are usually about 32cm (13in) long - bigger than most people's feet.

This is what some people think the Yeti, or Bigfoot, might look like. It is much bigger than a human, and covered in shaggy hair.

Peaceful places

People who want a peaceful life often go to live in the mountains. Monks are men who spend their lives praying and learning about their religion. They live in buildings called monasteries, which are often built on mountains. There, the monks can live in peace and quiet, far away from noisy towns.

Monastery

The picture on the right shows a monastery in the Pindus mountains in Greece. It is built on a high pillar of rock.

Mountains in danger

Mountains are usually far away from the busy areas where most people live, but mountain plants and animals are still in danger from some of the things that people do, such as chopping down trees and hunting. Even in areas where there are very few people, pollution carried in the air can destroy habitats and kill wildlife. Today, many people are trying to protect mountain areas and the wildlife living there from these dangers.

Endangered species

Plants and animals that are in danger of dying out are called endangered species. Many mountain species are endangered because the forests where they live are chopped down to make room for farms or houses. Some mountain animals are hunted by people for their skins, or for other parts of their bodies. People also pick plants and flowers for collections, or to make medicines.

Snow leopards are endangered because people hunt them for their fur, although this is against the law. Some snow leopards are kept in zoos, where they can live safely and breed. This helps them to increase their numbers. It is called captive breeding.

Snow leopard

Radio tracking

Scientists need to learn about wildlife before they can protect it. One way of finding out how animals live is by following, or tracking, their movements. These pictures show how a scientist tracks a snow leopard.

The scientist drugs the snow leopard to make it go to sleep for a short time. While it is asleep, a radio collar is fastened around its neck.

When the snow leopard wakes up and starts to move around, the transmitter on the collar sends out invisible radio signals through the air.

The scientist uses a receiver to pick up these signals. The receiver makes beeping noises. By listening to these, the scientist can tell where the snow leopard is.

Trees in trouble

People cut down trees for wood, or so they can use the land for farming. Cutting down large areas of forest is called deforestation. On mountains, this can be especially dangerous. The trees' roots hold soil in place on the mountainside. If the trees are cut down, rain can wash the soil down the mountain causing landslides. It may also block rivers and cause floods.

This picture shows a mountainside in Nepal. Many trees have been cut down, so there is nothing to stop the rain from washing away the soil. Once the soil has gone, the land is no good for growing crops.

In the 1970s, women in Nepal and India hugged trees to stop other people from cutting them down. This was called the Chipko movement. Soon, people in other countries began to do the same thing.

Pollution on the move

Forests, rivers and lakes can be damaged by acid rain and snow. These are caused by pollution, which may come from cities many miles away.

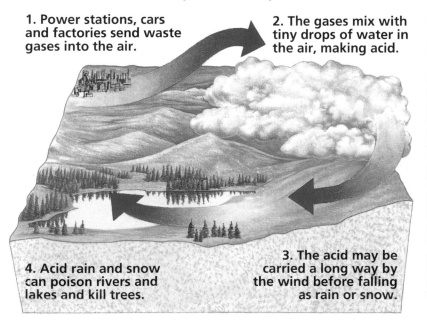

1. Power stations, cars and factories send waste gases into the air.

2. The gases mix with tiny drops of water in the air, making acid.

3. The acid may be carried a long way by the wind before falling as rain or snow.

4. Acid rain and snow can poison rivers and lakes and kill trees.

Protecting wildlife

Many groups of people are working to protect mountain areas and the plants and animals living there. They try to save endangered species, and to stop hunting, pollution and deforestation. In some places, areas have been set aside where it is against the law to hunt animals or chop down trees. These protected areas are called wildlife parks or reserves.

These American children are protesting against the destruction of redwood forests. Redwoods are a kind of conifer tree.

Joining a group is one way of helping to protect animals and plants. Some groups have special wildlife clubs for children. People from anywhere in the world can join. Here are some addresses you can write to:

Young
Ornithologists' Club,
RSPB,
The Lodge,
Sandy,
Bedfordshire SG19 2DL,
UK

Go Wild! Club,
WWF,
Panda House,
Weyside Park,
Godalming,
Surrey GU7 1XR,
UK

World Wildlife Fund,
90 Eglington Ave. East,
Toronto,
Ontario M4P 2Z7,
Canada

Lifewatch,
London Zoo,
Regents Park,
London NW1 4RY,
UK

Index

Acknowledgements

Photo on page 5, © WWF/Thor Larsen. Satellite photo of ozone hole on page 31, courtesy of NASA. All other photos in Part One, © Bryan & Cherry Alexander. Photo of Kayapo Indians on page 60, © Steve Cox/Survival International. Photo of Penan girl on page 60, © Robin Hanbury-Tenison/Survival International. Photo of Yanomami gathering bananas on page 60, © Peter Frey/Survival International. Photos of Yanomami on pages 60, 61, 63, © Victor Engelbert 1980/Survival International. Photo of National Park rangers on page 63, © Jose Kalpers/IGCP. Photos of cattle herders and of mother and child on page 92, © Sean Sprague/Panos Pictures. Photos of woman milking goat and of inside a Maasai house on page 92, © Neil Cooper/ Panos Pictures. Photo of woman carrying firewood on page 93, © WWF/ John Newby. Photo of men dancing on page 93, © Tony Souter/Hutchison Library. Photo of girl dressed for wedding on page 93, © Steve Turner/Oxford Scientific Films. Photo of Sherpa children on page 124, © Joan Klatchko/Hutchison Library. Photo of Sherpa porters on page 124, © Timothy Beddow/Hutchison Library. Photo of Chipko woman on page 127, © R. Berridale-Johnson/Panos Pictures. Photo of children demonstrating on page 127, © Daniel Dancer/STILL PICTURES. Survival International logo on page 63, © Survival International. WWF logo on pages 63 and 127, © WWF. ICBP logo on page 63, © ICBP. RSPB logo on page 127, © RSPB. Lifewatch logo on page 127, © Lifewatch.